"Do you find me pleasing, Dara?" Ricardo asked.

"Yes," she said softly.

"Do you want to know how I find you?" He stood unmoving in a pool of light. "But I think you already know. just as you knew when I pulled you off your horse in the tall grass and drew you against me like an animal in need. I can still hear the soft, keening sounds you made deep in your throat."

"I don't . . . remember."

"You kept saying, 'Ricardo, *querido*, I love you.' You arched up against me and our hands were all over each other. I wanted to take you then and there."

She felt the muscles of her stomach clench help-lessly and a burning deep within her. "Why didn't you?"

His fingertips caressed her cheek. "Because you're my lady, and you must have satin sheets and a chamber scented with lilac and lavender. So I came to you tonight." His hand moved to her neck. "As I will always come to you."

She gazed up at him, mesmerized. Dear heaven, she could actually smell the flowers. This was her lover who had risked everything so that she might have a night to remember. "Why?" she whispered.

"Because we were meant to be together." His hands slid her gown down to reveal creamy shoulders. "You belong to me." His touch set her skin afire. "And I belong to you. . . ."

WHAT ARE *LOVESWEPT* ROMANCES?

They are stories of true romance and touching emotion. We believe those two very important ingredients are constants in our highly sensual and very believable stories in the *LOVESWEPT* line. Our goal is to give you, the reader, stories of consistently high quality that may sometimes make you laugh, sometimes make you cry, but are always fresh and creative and contain many delightful surprises within their pages.

Most romance fans read an enormous number of books. Those they truly love, they keep. Others may be traded with friends and soon forgotten. We hope that each *LOVESWEPT* romance will be a treasure—a "keeper." We will always try to publish

*LOVE STORIES YOU'LL NEVER FORGET
BY AUTHORS YOU'LL ALWAYS REMEMBER*

The Editors

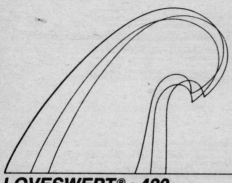

LOVESWEPT® • 420

Iris Johansen
Tender Savage

BANTAM BOOKS
NEW YORK • TORONTO • LONDON • SYDNEY • AUCKLAND

TENDER SAVAGE

A Bantam Book / September 1990

*LOVESWEPT® and the wave device are registered
trademarks of Bantam Books, a division of
Bantam Doubleday Dell Publishing Group, Inc.
Registered in U.S. Patent
and Trademark Office and elsewhere.*

*If you would be interested in receiving protective vinyl
covers for your Loveswept books, please write to this
address for information:*

> *Loveswept*
> *Bantam Books*
> *P. O. Box 985*
> *Hicksville, NY 11802*

ISBN 0-553-44051-9

Published simultaneously in the United States and Canada

---

*Bantam Books are published by Bantam Books, a division
of Bantam Doubleday Dell Publishing Group, Inc. Its trademark, consisting of the words "Bantam Books" and the
portrayal of a rooster, is Registered in U.S. Patent and
Trademark Office and in other countries. Marca Regis-
trada. Bantam Books, 666 Fifth Avenue, New York, New
York 10103*

PRINTED IN THE UNITED STATES OF AMERICA

OPM   0 9 8 7 6 5 4 3 2 1

One

"It will be dangerous, Miss Clavel," Paco said gravely. "I won't lie to you. You could be raped or tortured, even killed."

Lara Clavel tried to hide her shiver of fear from Paco Renalto's keen gaze. In the short time she had been in the major's tent, she had learned that there was a great deal more to Renalto than elfin features and an air of insouciance. He had a sharp, probing intelligence. She shouldn't have been surprised. He couldn't have risen to be Ricardo Lázaro's second in command with only puckish charm to recommend him. She forced a smile. "I really wish you wouldn't tell me about all these dire things that could happen. I'm scared enough already."

"You have to be warned. Ricardo wouldn't permit you to go into such a dangerous situation without your knowing full well what it might cost you. I can't either."

"Not even to save the leader of your great revolution?" Lara's tone was deliberately flippant.

"Not even then." A sudden smile lit Paco Renalto's face. "You cannot choose without knowing the facts, and that's what this revolution is all about. Ricardo wouldn't thank me for discarding those principles just to save his life."

"No? I find that hard to believe. Self-preservation is the first law of nature."

"Some things are worth dying for." Paco paused. "And so are some people. I'd give my life for Ricardo Lázaro."

And so would a hundred thousand other revolutionaries on this blasted island in the Caribbean, Lara thought wearily. The man seemed capable of hypnotizing everyone who came in contact with him. Lázaro was not only a brilliant military strategist, but the most charismatic of leaders, and the war he had waged against the Communist junta on Saint Pierre had made headlines around the world for the last nine years. It wasn't often a figure as dashing as Lázaro came on the scene, and the media had made the most of every opportunity to capitalize on the general's magnetism. Five years ago Lázaro had smuggled his book *Right to Choose* out of Saint Pierre and it had become a worldwide best-seller acclaimed both for its philosophy and for its poetic style. A poet and a warrior. How was anyone supposed to fight against a combination like that? She just wished Brett hadn't been one of those thousands to fall under his spell. She looked intently into Paco Renalto's eyes. "Yet you caution me against risking my own life for the man."

"You're not one of us. You're an American and you've told me yourself you have no sympathy for our cause." Paco leaned back in his camp chair. "I've been with Ricardo since we were students together at the university. He's closer than a brother to me."

Brett had been with the revolutionaries for only six months and he expressed the same kind of loyalty to Lázaro—loyalty that had landed him in a wheelchair in a clinic in Barbados. "I don't have to be one of Ricardo Lázaro's so-called adorers to help him escape from prison. You said yourself that the fact I'm not a citizen of Saint Pierre is in my favor. The junta's secret police has no record or fingerprints on file for me."

"True." Paco gazed at her thoughtfully. "We could falsify your documents to make sure you appear to be a vulnerable target to Jurado."

"Jurado?"

"Captain Emilio Jurado. He commands the security police at the Abbey. You've heard of the Abbey?"

"Yes." Everyone in the world knew of the security prison known as the Abbey. Formerly a religious monastery, it had been converted into one of the most horrendous political prisons in the world. Human rights organizations were constantly condemning the atrocities reported to take place there.

"That's where they're keeping Ricardo. He's been there for over five months."

Lara flinched and her grasp tightened on the wooden arms of her chair. She should have known they'd keep a prisoner of Lázaro's importance at that hellish place. Dear heaven, what was she doing sitting there in the middle of a military stronghold trying to talk Renalto into letting her help free Lázaro? She wasn't one of those tough guerrilla women she had seen as she had been led through the camp. She hated even the thought of war. "I'm surprised that Lázaro's still alive if he's been at the Abbey that long."

"They stopped torturing him after the first few weeks. They knew he wouldn't break and they didn't want to make a martyr of Ricardo by killing him." Paco's lips tightened grimly. "However, they still hope to damage his image by forcing him to betray us. Jurado's been coming at him from another angle for the last month."

What kind of man could withstand weeks of torture inflicted by men more sophisticated in the art of cruelty than the priests of the Spanish Inquisition, Lara wondered. "How do you know all this?"

"We have a man at the Abbey. He's one of Jurado's officers. We couldn't get him in the cell block, but he works in Jurado's office and is occasionally able to exert a certain influence." Paco looked down at the papers on his desk. "Why are you willing to help us, Miss Clavel?"

"Lara," she corrected. "And I told you why."

He nodded. "I knew your brother well. He's a brave man."

"He's an idealistic idiot who fell under Lázaro's spell like all the rest of you," she said bluntly. "And look where it got him."

"And you don't consider yourself an idealist?"

"Of course not. I'm as hardheaded as they come. The only reason I'm here is that I know the moment they release my brother from the hospital he'll be back here on this godforsaken island trying to rescue Lázaro from that prison." She gestured impatiently. "The doctors say he needs another six months of outpatient therapy, but there's no way he'll do it. If I don't get Lázaro out of prison before he's released, he'll be hobbling down here on crutches."

"And that's the only reason?"

She was silent a moment longer before she admitted reluctantly, "I owe Ricardo Lázaro. My brother told me your fearless leader was captured because he led the team that rescued Brett's platoon when they were overrun by the enemy."

"That's true." Paco smiled faintly. "But Ricardo saved many American lives that night, and the members of those men's families didn't come rushing down to save his neck."

"I pay my debts." She met his gaze. "Will you use me or not?"

He gazed at her a long moment. "I don't like it."

"But you'll do it?"

"Yes." Paco's smile faded. "The war has come to a standstill without Ricardo. We need someone in that prison, and getting a woman in will be far easier, according to what our man at the Abbey tells us." He shrugged. "As I said, I don't like it, but for the good of Saint Pierre we're forced into many decisions we don't like."

"The good of Saint Pierre or the good of Ricardo Lázaro?"

"Ricardo Lázaro *is* Saint Pierre." For an instant Renalto's face was illuminated with the same expression Lara had seen on her brother's face when he had spoken of Lázaro. "You'll realize that when you meet him."

"If I don't get killed first," she said lightly.

Paco didn't smile.

"I was joking."

"I know. You're frightened and you think to hide it with laughter."

"I'm not frightened. I'm just—" She broke off as she met his gaze. "Well, perhaps a little."

"It's all right to be frightened." Paco leaned forward and gently covered her hand with his own. "We'll do all we can to protect you. If it's any comfort to you, Ricardo is worth any risk."

She moistened her dry lips with her tongue. "I'm not sure anyone is worth this kind of risk. I don't even know why I'm doing this. Brett inherited all the swashbuckler qualities in the family. I'm not at all brave."

"No?" He smiled curiously. "It wasn't easy for you to come to a war-torn country like Saint Pierre, and it must have been even harder to find someone to bring you to me. Perhaps you're braver than you think."

She shook her head. "I'm only doing what I have to do. There's nothing brave about that." She straightened her shoulders and continued briskly, "Now, tell me what I have to do to get Lázaro out of that prison."

"You won't like it." His gaze focused soberly on her face. "And you'll have to do it alone. If you told Ricardo what we're planning, he wouldn't let you make—"

"Dear me, are you taking away Lázaro's 'right to choose'?" she asked with a touch of mockery.

"Yes, and he'll curse me for it." He shook his head wearily. "But we *need* him."

"Then stop warning me and tell me how to get your god out of the Abbey."

"Ricardo isn't a—" He stopped and shrugged. "Ricardo has to be experienced. You'll see."

There was no question of that fact, Lara thought grimly. If Renalto's plan worked, she was sure she would see considerably more of Ricardo Lázaro than would make her comfortable.

The woman was barefoot.

Ricardo Lázaro's hands tightened on the bars of the window as he watched Jurado propel the woman across the courtyard from the direction of his office. It was close to noon and the flagstones must have been burning hot beneath the soles of the woman's small feet. Why the hell hadn't the bastard given her shoes to wear?

Lord, he had been here too long. Why was he worrying about the woman's lack of shoes when she would soon probably be suffering far more pain? Jurado seldom gave a prisoner his august personal attention unless there was information to be extracted.

The woman looked to be little more than a child, he thought with compassion, small and fine boned with long fair hair of a shade somewhere between tan and gold. Jurado's goon squad must have torn her from her bed, for she wore only a loose white cotton-gauze gown with a high round neck that buttoned down the front.

She wore nothing beneath the gown.

And she wasn't a child.

As she drew closer, he could see the generous swell of her breasts pressing against the bodice of the gown and glimpsed the dark pink of her nipples through the sheer cotton gauze. The blood rushed to his groin in an arousal as involuntary as it was primitive. He closed his eyes so that he could no longer see her. Self-disgust poured through him, and his hands tightened on the bars as he struggled to subdue his physical response. He was no mind-less animal to lust after Jurado's prisoner. He should be feeling only sympathy and anger for the poor woman.

He opened his eyes and the lust was still there.

She was a woman of gold, he mused. Her skin was a rich honey shade, glowing with silky health. She walked with a springy grace that caused the gauzy gown to flow sensually around her hips, revealing the dark shadow of her womanhood. His gaze lingered on that shadow in helpless fascination as he felt the thick throb in his loins intensify until it became pain. Jurado had almost reached the door of the cell block and she stood in the courtyard, only yards away from Ricardo. He saw her hesitate, tense, brace herself as the door of the block swung open. She was very frightened.

Suddenly the lust dominating Ricardo was joined by another sensation just as powerful. He felt an agonizing need to protect her from what she had to face beyond that door.

Jurado pushed her inside the cell block and the door closed behind them.

Ricardo's teeth clenched in frustration. Control. The isolation he had suffered had made every reaction and emotion painfully sharp. He couldn't let himself be torn apart like this or Jurado would win. He wouldn't have survived physical torture only to be defeated in the psychological battle the captain was now waging.

He heard the sound of boots on the flagstones of the hall and unconsciously tensed. No other pris-oner occupied this section of the block and he knew those steps. He had come to recognize them, wait for them, during those endless weeks of torture. Jurado was bringing the woman here.

He should have guessed Jurado's purpose, but this woman didn't have the voluptuous appeal of the others the captain had chosen. Yet, as he remembered the sensual delicacy of her body, he felt again a stirring he knew Jurado would notice if he turned away from the window to face him.

"I have something for you, Lázaro." The door swung open behind him and he heard Jurado thrust the woman forward into the cell. "A pretty little pullet to while away the long hours. Turn around and look at her."

Ricardo's spine stiffened, but he didn't move. His senses were so acutely aroused that even across the wide space separating them he could hear the light, rapid sound of her breathing and could catch her heady, sweet fragrance. With effort he kept his tone light and mocking. "Again, Jurado? I should think you'd give up. Do you consider the third time lucky?"

"Ah, but this one is different. I admit I made a mistake in judgment before. I should have known those other whores would never tempt a man of your discrimination. I thought their extraordinary talents might be an inducement that would make you overlook—"

"You're wasting your time. I don't need a woman."

"Oh, but you do." Jurado must have pushed the woman forward because her scent was stronger. "Though your followers claim you have superhuman powers of self-control and self-discipline, you're a man like any other. A very earthy man. Our informants tell us you generally require a woman several times a week." He added softly, "And it's been more than five months, Lázaro."

"I really didn't notice." Ricardo's lips twisted sardonically. "You've made every moment of my stay here at the Abbey so very entertaining."

"We need to know the location of your arms cache." Jurado shrugged. "We didn't think torture would break you, but we had to try."

"And you enjoyed every minute of it."

"Of course. You've evaded us for over eight years. By the time we captured you, I had a great deal of frustration to release. Frustration is a terrible thing, isn't it, Lázaro? And sexual frustration is more terrible than any other for a man. Now turn around and look at her. She's clean and pretty and her hair shines like sunlight."

Ricardo released the bars and carefully kept his gaze from the woman as he slowly turned to face Jurado. "And no doubt you found her in the same bordello as you did the others."

"No, this one's a prisoner, just like you." Jurado touched the shining wing of hair at the woman's temple. "Her name's Lara Albert. She was picked up at the airport trying to leave the country with several thousand dollars in our currency. She said no one told her our currency was not allowed out of Saint Pierre." He added in English, "Say hello to the gentleman, Lara."

The woman remained silent.

Again in English he asked, "Don't you wish to greet the great hero of the revolution? How rude of you, my dear." Jurado gently stroked her hair back from her face. "You'll have to teach her better manners, Lázaro."

Ricardo felt a sudden fierce surge of rage as he saw Jurado's hand stroking her. Lord, what was wrong with him? He carefully masked his expression. "You don't need trouble with the United States. Let her go."

"Actually, we were considering releasing her before I realized how valuable she could be. She was sent here to the Abbey until a decision could be made." A smile lit his round, boyish face. "She's only a secretary and her passport lists no next of kin. No one knows she's been arrested. She offers us little diplomatic risk."

"Why run any risk at all?"

Jurado ignored the question. "She's entirely at your disposal, of course. Anything you wish to do to or with her is up to you. I'm afraid you'll have to speak English with her to make your needs known. She understands very little Spanish." He trailed off as his gaze locked with Ricardo's. "She's a virgin. Isn't that remarkable in this day and age? Our physicians were quite startled during the examination they gave her when she was admitted to the Abbey this morning. Startled and stimulated. A man always likes to be first, and I had trouble keeping them off her. But one of my officers suggested she might be of value to us with you, and I knew at once that he was right."

"No, he was wrong."

Jurado shook his head. "You like Americans and you have the true soul of a knight. Obviously, such a man would be attracted to a helpless virgin. Why won't you look at her? She's a lovely little thing. Fine bones, pretty breasts, and that skin . . ." He sighed. "I truly envy you, Lázaro. Can't you see she's trembling with eagerness for the pleasure you can give her?"

Ricardo tried to keep his gaze from wandering toward the woman. "If she's trembling, it's from fear, and I've never found terror in a woman an aph-rodisiac. Get her out of here."

"Oh, no. She stays here with you," Jurado said. "She'll share your meals, your conversation, and your cot. I've always found propinquity to be a pow-erful spur." His gaze moved to Ricardo's lower body. "Particularly to a man in your state. I see the little one arouses you."

The bastard. Ricardo felt a jolt of welcome anger that temporarily submerged the lust pounding through him. "So did your whores. It's a natural response." He smiled crookedly. "But I've learned to control my body. I have no intention of letting you gain a weapon to use on me. You might as well give up now, Jurado."

Jurado turned and moved toward the door. "We shall see. I'll give you time to change your mind." He paused to look back over his shoulder. "But I admit I'm a little impatient. If you don't follow your natural inclinations within a reasonable length of time, I'll take her from you and give her to the guards to enjoy." He smiled as he saw the flicker of anger on Ricardo's face. "You see, I do understand you, Lázaro. You have the misfortune of being an idealist, a protector of the weak and the innocent. Well, I give you an innocent to protect and enjoy at one and the same time. What more could you ask?" His gaze shifted to Lara. "A gang rape isn't pleasant, my dear. You'd better make yourself very appealing to our great liberator." He slammed the door behind him and an instant later Ricardo heard the guard turn the key in the lock.

Ricardo turned back to the window and stared blindly out at the courtyard. Lord, he didn't need this. His hands reached out and again grasped the bars at the window, the muscles of his upper arms distending as his grip tightened. He wanted to break something. He felt helpless and frustrated and as hot as a beardless adolescent in the first throes of passion.

He slowly forced his hands to relax on the bars. Nothing could be done about the situation and it would do no good to frighten the woman by a show of violence. She had probably gone through enough already at Jurado's hands.

"It's all right," he said. "I won't hurt you." He gazed at Jurado strolling across the courtyard toward his office and thought how pleasant a sight it would be to see that small, dapper figure ignited by a flamethrower. "And evidently the junta's pride and joy is giving you a reprieve from whatever he'd planned for you."

"I notice you're not saying I won't have to worry after the reprieve."

Her voice was low and faintly tremulous, and its femininity stroked and aroused him as much as that first sight of her. He felt the muscles of his stomach clench and then knot painfully. It was only sex, he told himself. Sex had nothing to do with his mind or emotions. A man of will and intelligence could subdue even that most powerful and primitive of urges. "I don't believe in lying. Jurado will do what he likes with you. He's commandant of the Abbey and uses gang rape frequently as an interrogation tool." He kept his tone deliberately matter-of-fact. "I can't stop him from hurting you, but I can show you ways to make the pain less. We have a little time and you can learn enough to—"

"Is that a microphone?"

He turned and followed her glance to the small

black metal object mounted high on a shelf in the corner of the room.

"Yes, the Abbey isn't sophisticated enough for video surveillance, but Jurado likes to make me feel the lack of privacy." He raised his voice. "Don't you, Jurado?"

"It's *terrible*." Her voice was shrill. "Everything here is hideous. How can they do this to me? I'm frightened and angry. I'm no whore to be—" She broke off. "And now you tell me they can hear us while we—" Her voice rose hysterically. "Well, I won't have it. I won't!" She ran across the room to the washbasin and grabbed the water pitcher. She slung it at the microphone, knocking the device from its shelf and splattering both it and the white stucco wall with water. The smashed microphone crackled and hissed as it dangled on its long cord.

"That won't do any good," Ricardo said gently. "They'll just replace it."

"Is that the only bug?"

"Yes, it's not really a security device. Jurado only installed it to annoy me."

"Tape recorders?"

"No."

"How long do we have?" Her voice was breathless, but no longer hysterical.

He slowly stiffened, his gaze narrowing on her face. "Jurado should be here in five minutes. Perhaps less."

"The guards in the cell block?"

"They'll wait for Jurado unless there's a threat of escape. They know he likes to run the show."

She flew across the room toward him and spoke quickly in a whisper. "Paco Renalto."

He repeated warily, "Paco?"

"He sent me to tell you they'll be attacking the Abbey day after tomorrow. He wants you to be ready."

"Ready? I've been ready for over five months." Ricardo felt a leap of hope he quickly smothered. "You expect me to believe you? Jurado delivers you to my bed and suddenly I find you're working for Paco?" He shook his head. "Not likely."

"You've got to believe me. We don't have much time." Lara moistened her lips with her tongue and whispered, "Renalto said to mention the caverns."

Ricardo's hand automatically clapped across her lips. "Quiet!"

Lara turned her head to avoid his hand. "I won't say any more about it. I don't even know what it means. Renalto just said to use it as a password."

Ricardo was thinking quickly. The Abbey had been breached before by frequent raids but not in the last few years. The grounds were now well guarded and enclosed by an electric wire fence, and even if the courtyard were reached, there were still problems. The Abbey was a one-story U-shaped building and the cells were all on the left side of the courtyard. He shook his head. "The cell block's too well guarded for him to hit. There's a machine gun mounted on the roof above Jurado's office aimed at this side of the courtyard. How does he intend to—"

"How do I know?" Lara's lashes quickly lowered to veil her eyes. "He just sent me here to tell you to be ready."

"Who *are* you?"

"That doesn't matter. I'm here to help." She laughed shakily. "Though at the moment I can't think why. I never expected to playact as some kind of sacrificial virgin when I came to Saint Pierre. It's not my style at all. I've always been very sensible and practical." She tilted her head as she heard the sharp clatter of footsteps on the flagstones in the hall. "They're coming. Tell me, do they give you pencil and paper?"

He shook his head. "And the only time we'll be able to talk freely is when we're taken to the showers. None of the guards or officers speak English except Jurado, but I never know when he's listening."

"Showers? When is that? Never mind, there's no time." She dashed across the cell, threw herself on the cot, and turned her face to the wall, curling up in fetal position just as Jurado burst into the cell followed by two guards.

Jurado's cheeks were livid with fury as he looked down at Lara's cringing form. "You disappoint me." He strode to the cot, grabbed Lara's arm, and jerked her to a sitting position on the cot. "No man likes an hysterical woman. Get hold of yourself."

"I don't want to be here." Lara whimpered. "I can't stay with him. I don't know what to do. Can't I—"

Jurado's palm cracked against her cheek.

She cried out as her head snapped back from the force of the blow.

"That's enough, Jurado." Ricardo took an impulsive step forward, his hands clenching into fists at his sides. "Can't you see she's too frightened to know what she's doing?"

"Then she'll have to learn." Jurado took a step back from Lara, and the annoyance disappeared from his demeanor as he saw Ricardo's expression. He nodded approvingly. "It goes well. Your protective instincts are already aroused and you've barely met the girl. What will you feel after you've taken her to bed?" He motioned to the microphone one of the guards was examining. "How long will it take to fix that?"

"It will have to be replaced. I have to remove this one and then go to the storeroom and get another one." The man shrugged. "Perhaps an hour."

"Then do it. I have an idea we may hear some very erotic sounds coming from this cell in the next few days." Jurado glanced back at Ricardo. "And then I'll have you, Lázaro."

Ricardo didn't trust himself to speak. He should have remained silent when Jurado had struck her, but rage and possessiveness had risen like a red haze. Possessiveness? The thought sent a chill through him. "She means nothing to me," he said without intonation. "Do what you wish with her."

"I will." Jurado strode toward the door. "And with you, my fine rebel."

Lara forced herself to remain quiet until the guard disconnected the broken microphone and left the cell.

"What's this all about?" She sat on the cot, her hands folded in her lap, her gaze on the rigid line of Ricardo's spine. He had turned his back to her again and she could sense he was trying to distance himself from her, as he had done when she had entered the cell. "Oh, Renalto told me the reason he thought Jurado would throw us together, but I don't understand it. Why does Jurado want us to—" She stopped and then started again, "I mean, I would guess that the junta doesn't permit prisoners—"

"Sex?" He turned to face her and she found herself experiencing the same ripple of shock that had surged through her when she had first entered his cell. Ricardo Lázaro was different from what Lara had expected him to be. She had seen newspaper photos of him, but they had only depicted his classic good looks, the glossy dark hair with just a hint of curl, the glittering intensity of the ebony eyes. The pictures had failed to reveal the burning vitality, the air of controlled power he exuded. Ricardo's hair flowed past his shoulders and his green army fatigues were faded, ragged, and hung loose on his six-foot frame. Yet the man stood arrow straight and the bearing of his slender, sinewy body was quietly indomitable. "Sex is only a tool for Jurado. He believes I'll feel affection for a woman who shares my bed. He wants a weapon to use against me."

"How?"

"Torture. Jurado didn't succeed in getting the information he needs by torturing me, so he thinks to win the day by using someone else's pain against me. It's a common practice here to torture a man's family before his eyes to make him break." He smiled bitterly. "I wouldn't follow his advice about making yourself appealing to me. It could prove very painful."

"More painful than being gang raped?"

"That would probably come first," Ricardo said quietly. "With me forced to watch—if Jurado was convinced you meant something to me."

She shivered. "I feel like a piece of meat in a butcher shop." Both the words and the shiver were genuine. What kind of world bred men like Jurado who used human beings as pawns? "I'm no side of beef and I'm no harem girl, and I hate being treated like either one. I'll make damn sure you don't find me attractive, even if I have to make a eunuch of you."

A slow smile lit his hard face with surprising sweetness. "That's the spirit." He grimaced ruefully. "Though I'd appreciate you not being so enthusiastic about ridding me of that particular body part." He moved across the cell toward her. "Your cheek is bruised." His palm moved caressingly on the soft marked flesh and she felt a sudden hot tingle explode through her body. "I've already caused you pain. I'm sorry, Lara."

Jurado had said Ricardo Lázaro was an earthy man, and now she could see that earthiness in his expression—the sensual heaviness of his lower lip, the flush that mantled his lean cheeks, the rapid drumming of the pulse in the hollow of his strong brown throat. She found herself unable to look away from that throbbing betrayal.

Her voice sounded oddly breathless even to her own ears. "It . . . doesn't hurt anymore."

"No?" His fingers lingered on her flesh, his gaze holding her own. The air in the cell seemed to become heavier and charged with electricity. She couldn't breathe and she couldn't look away. She felt as if she were waiting for a storm to break.

"That's good." His hand dropped away from her cheek. "I wish I could say I could keep away any pain that might hurt you, but I can't do that, Lara. I can't betray—" He broke off and drew a deep breath. "If something goes wrong, I can't let your pain matter to me."

"I know that." At last she managed to tear her gaze away from him. "And I have no intention of allowing myself to be hurt by that greasy pig. Paco Renalto and the rest of your army may be fanatics, but I've absolutely no inclination toward martyrdom."

His gravity vanished and his lips twitched with suppressed humor. "Then may I suggest you've definitely involved yourself in the wrong situation? Why the devil are you here?"

"I owed you a debt." As he continued to stand there looking at her, she shrugged. "My brother is Brett Clavel. He was a sergeant in the platoon that—"

"I know Brett," he interrupted.

"I wasn't sure you'd remember him." She looked away from him. "A lot of Americans flocked down here to fight for you."

"Not for me, for Saint Pierre," he corrected softly. "And for the right to choose."

Her hands tightened on her lap. "No, for *you*," she said fiercely. "You're the Pied Piper. Do you think Brett would have left college and come down here to fight for Paco Renalto? Brett thinks you can walk on water. He could have been killed, dammit."

"You resent me," he observed, his gaze searching her expression.

"Brett is all I've ever had. I won't have him killed or maimed because he's dazzled by you. He doesn't belong here."

"And neither do you."

"I had to come. You saved his life."

He smiled crookedly. "Yet you hold me responsible for endangering it in the first place."

"It was the only way to—" She stopped and drew a deep breath. "I suppose I really came because I want a promise from you."

"I'm afraid I'm not in a position to grant promises at present."

"You will be, when you're free." She gazed up at

him. "When Brett comes back to Saint Pierre, I want you to promise to send him away."

He became still. "A man must make his own decisions."

"Not this one. What's one more soldier to you?"

"One more soldier is nothing. But one more man is everything. I won't interfere with your brother's right to choose his own path."

"The right to choose." She smiled bitterly. "I don't care about your damn philosophy. I want my brother safe."

"I want all my brothers safe," Ricardo said tiredly. "Safe in their homes, away from the sound of guns. Someday it will happen perhaps." He sat down on the cot beside her. "I can't give you my promise, Lara."

Dear heaven, he was hard as nails. Yet his expression in this moment wasn't hard at all. He only looked sad and discouraged and weary, and she felt an infinitesimal softening toward him. But she mustn't soften, she told herself desperately. She had to convince him to give her his word. "Then I'll just have to keep at you until you do."

The weariness in his expression vanished as he smiled at her. "I've never known a woman to go to these lengths to accomplish what she wanted. Are you always this determined?"

She nodded briskly. "You don't get anywhere unless you set a goal and stick to it."

"You've found that out through long years of labor and experimentation, no doubt. How old are you, Lara?"

She was annoyed by his indulgent tone. "Older than I look. People always think I'm younger because I'm small."

"How old?"

"Twenty-one."

Ricardo swore softly under his breath. "And Paco sent you here?"

"Brett is my twin and you had no compunction about accepting him into your damned army. Why should Renalto quibble about using me?"

"In the military, you have a chance. The Abbey is different."

She swallowed, her annoyance banished by the panic that flooded through her. "Renalto thinks we have a chance to escape."

"Maybe." His gaze searched her face. "Why the hell didn't someone stop you? Don't you have any family?"

She shook her head. "My parents were divorced, and my mother died when we were twelve. My father couldn't be bothered with children and took off for parts unknown right after the funeral. Brett and I spent the next four years in foster homes." She shrugged. "What difference does my background make? I would have come anyway. Don't women have the right to choose, too, in your brave new world?"

"Yes." He grimaced. "But men also have the right to choose to try to protect them."

She gazed at him in astonishment for an instant before she suddenly chuckled. "A sort of liberated sexism?"

"I never said my philosophy was foolproof against basic human drives."

She shook her head, a smile still lingering on her lips. The man was not only bigger than life, he was completely disarming. "Well, the basic drive we should be focusing on now is surviving until we can get out of here."

A frown wrinkled his brow. "I can't understand why Paco sent you into a place like this just to warn me."

Her smile faded and she looked away from him. "He wanted you to be prepared."

"It's too great a risk for you." He stood up and moved restlessly toward the window again. "Lord, two days is a long time."

"Not when you consider you've already been here for more than five months."

"I wasn't penned in a ten-by-six-foot cell with a half-dressed woman for those five months," he said tightly. "Jurado's not stupid. He knows I'm horny as hell."

Lara felt the hot color suffuse her entire body. Everywhere the gauze of her gown touched, her flesh was on fire with sensation. She could feel her breasts swell, the nipples harden with arousal at his words as well as the picture they evoked.

"Look, I'm sorry." He didn't look at her; his voice was low, the words measured. "You don't have to be afraid of me. I won't hurt you. It's just that I find you . . . desirable. If you'll help me, we'll get along fine for the next two days."

"I'll help you." Her voice was shaking and she carefully steadied it. "It's a difficult situation and I don't see why we can't be companionable."

"Don't you?" He laughed shortly. "I could make you see why with the speed of light if I—" He broke off, and when he spoke again, his voice was once more controlled. "You're right; there's no reason." He paused. "The guard should be back with the microphone any minute, so listen to me very carefully. Any conversation will have to be general; never mention names or places. Don't argue with the guards; just do as they tell you to do. They're afraid of Jurado, but they're not above an occasional cuff or kick if you annoy them. Okay?"

She nodded. "I won't do anything to endanger our chances. I want out of here as much as you do."

He lifted his gaze from the flagstone floor and smiled at her. "You look like a solemn little girl." His smile vanished as his glance shifted to her breasts swelling beneath their veil of gauze. "Almost."

Her eyes widened as she felt a hot liquid tingling start between her thighs. What was wrong with her? Every word, every gesture he made, evoked a physical response. "I . . . wish you wouldn't stare at me. It makes me feel uncomfortable."

"I've been trying not to look at you since you walked into the cell," he said thickly. "This damn hellhole's not very big and every time I look up I see—" He stopped, glancing at the door. "The guard's coming."

She had heard the footsteps, too, and felt a rush of relief. At least the presence of the microphone would put a barrier between them. Ricardo's effect on her both physically and emotionally was escalating by the moment into something most unsettling.

"Yes," Ricardo said softly.

She looked at him inquiringly.

His gaze was fastened on her face and his smile was knowing. "It will help for a little while but not for long. We'll have to rely on ourselves, *querida*."

How had he known what she was thinking? For a moment she could almost believe the legends his followers had woven about him. Nonsense, she quickly told herself. He was merely accustomed to reading body language, and no one could say she had a poker face. Brett had always said her every emotion was mirrored clear as glass.

"I've been relying on myself for a long time," she said quietly.

"So have I." The weariness was back and with it she had the vague impression of a deep and abiding loneliness. "But I think I'll be stretched to the limit this time."

Before she could answer, the key turned in the lock and the door swung open to admit the guard carrying the new microphone.

Two

It took the guard over an hour to replace the microphone and during that time Lara sat silent on the cot, every muscle stiff with tension. Lord, it was hot. The white stucco walls seemed to hold and breathe heat into the room like a giant oven. She could feel the perspiration beading the nape of her neck beneath the heavy length of her hair. How had Ricardo stood it all those months?

She glanced at him out of the corner of her eye. The heat didn't appear to be bothering him. He wasn't even sweating. He sat motionless on the floor beneath the window a few feet away from the cot, his hands looped loosely around his knees as he watched the short, black-mustached guard splicing the cord back into the socket of the microphone. Ricardo seemed totally absorbed by the procedure.

Lara's gaze shifted restlessly around the cell. There was little enough to see. The cell's interior was as stark and barren today as it must have been when occupied by the monks. The cot on which she was sitting contained only a meager pillow and a thin, lumpy mattress covered by a raw cotton sheet. The washstand across the room was occupied only by a cracked and stained blue washbowl. The sunlight streamed through the bars at the window, painting blocks of light on the flagstones of the floor before Ricardo and touching the curls falling over his forehead. She could see no trunk for personal possessions, no books, nothing to distract the mind from the deprivation to which Jurado had condemned his prisoner. Ricardo had said he wasn't even allowed pencil and paper, she remembered.

"How do you stand it here?" she asked abruptly.

Ricardo's glance shifted from the guard to her face. "This is the luxury suite compared to where they put me when I first came here. Jurado thinks he's pampering me at the moment. Every evening they take me down the hall to the bathroom and let me take a shower. I get to wash my clothes twice a week. They feed me once a day. What more could a man ask?"

"There's nothing to *do*."

He smiled. "They can't keep me from thinking. I plan campaigns, do memory exercises. I even compose poems."

"The poet-warrior," she murmured.

He made a face. "Media hype."

"The media certainly loves you," she agreed.

"Publicity helps the revolution. I have friends and backers in America and Europe who see that everyone knows what's going on here." His lips thinned. "You'd be surprised how few countries are willing to supply arms to the junta now that the spotlight of public opinion has been focused on places like the Abbey. Two years ago every cell here was filled. Now

Jurado only chances holding a favored few for his entertainment."

"So you let your backers exploit you."

"It's a small price to pay." He was silent a moment. "When I was a student at the university, I wanted to be a poet. I could see myself doing nothing for the rest of my life but writing beautiful words that would shake the world."

"Some people would say that your book did shake the world."

"Some people. Not you."

"I've never read your book. Not my cup of tea."

"What *is* your cup of tea, Lara?"

"I've never wanted to shake the world. I just want something of my own to hold on to. Someday I'm going to live in a small town and have a home by a lake and lots of dogs and a few close friends." She looked down at the floor. "I'm not the type of person who would ever start a revolution."

"I think you're wrong."

Her gaze lifted swiftly to see the faintest smile indenting the corners of Ricardo's lips as he said, "It's not the rabble-rousers who form the foundation of a revolution; it's the silent majority. If wood is ready to burn, it takes only a spark."

"And you think I'd take only a spark?"

He gazed at her thoughtfully. "I think a woman who would rush headlong into a situation like this has enough fire to set an entire country ablaze."

She swallowed and looked quickly across the room at the guard, who had completed the splicing and was plugging the cord into the socket. "He's almost done. We'll have to be careful what we say from now on."

"We haven't said anything that Jurado couldn't hear."

She realized with astonishment that what he said was true. Their conversation had been casual, almost impersonal, and yet she felt as if every word had been charged with meaning and intimacy.

"What do we do now?"

"Wait."

She slowly leaned back against the stucco wall. "I'm not very good at composing mental poems and I have a terrible memory. Can we talk?"

His gaze had shifted back to the guard. "If I don't have to look at you. Where the hell did you get that gown?"

Scorching heat flowed over her again. "They gave it to me at the infirmary after they . . . examined me."

"Oh, yes, the examination." Ricardo's clasped fingers tightened until the knuckles turned white. "Did they hurt you?"

"No, but they weren't exactly clinical." She laughed shakily. "They scared me."

The guard replaced the microphone on the shelf and switched it on. Without looking at either of them, he turned on his heel and strode from the cell.

Lara gazed in fascination at the small black box. She felt suddenly stripped, humiliated in a deeply personal way.

"Don't let it bother you," Ricardo said. "It doesn't really make you less than you are to have your privacy invaded." His dark eyes were suddenly twinkling. "On the contrary, you have to reach a certain stature before you have the dubious honor of having clods like Jurado try to make you feel this helpless."

It was the second time he had effortlessly guessed what she was thinking, but this time she felt no wariness, only gratitude. His light comment had banished the sense of defilement and made Jurado's listening presence seem pitiful and unimportant.

"You're the one with the stature." She wrinkled her nose. "I'm just along for the ride."

"Ride?" His eyes gleamed with reckless humor. "That's certainly what Jurado has in mind, but I had no idea you were in agreement."

The color flew to her cheeks as she caught the double entendre. Dammit, she seemed to be doing nothing but blushing since she had come into this cell. "You know I didn't—"

"I know," Ricardo interrupted, his smile vanishing. "Sorry, my mother was part Irish and sometimes the wild Celt gets the upper hand." His gaze went to the microphone. "I'm well aware you don't want to be here any more than I want you here."

He was trying to protect her, to banish any hint of intimacy Jurado might seize as a weapon. She knew what he was doing and yet the words still hurt her in some strange fashion. "I'm glad we understand each other."

"Yes." He wearily leaned his head back against the wall and closed his eyes. "There's no question we understand each other."

At twilight two guards came to take them to the bathroom and shower at the end of the corridor. One of the guards was the small, mustached soldier who had replaced the microphone and the other was taller, uglier, with broad cheekbones and a hooked nose.

Ricardo spoke urgently as they reached the bathroom. "It will be all right. Ignore them. They have orders not to touch you."

"What do—" She didn't finish the sentence as the taller guard opened the door and pushed her into the bathroom. Ricardo didn't follow, but the guard did, and she understood what he had been trying to tell her.

When she had finished using the bathroom, the grinning guard opened the door across the room and motioned for her to precede him. As she passed, he gave her a surreptitious, obscene caress, and she bolted into the shower room. She wished she had a blackjack to smash his sneering face. She wished she could make him feel as helpless and embarrassed as he had made her feel. She wished she could—

The shower cubicle across the room was obviously meant for one person and that person was already occupying it.

Lara moistened her lips with her tongue as she saw Ricardo standing naked beneath the spray. His skin was golden brown all over, his muscles corded and sinewy with power in spite of his leanness. A triangle of black hair thatched his chest, narrowing to a pencil-slim line at his waist before surrounding his manhood. She pulled her gaze quickly back to his face. "I didn't expect . . . this."

He smiled grimly. "Why not? Jurado said we were to do everything together."

The guard shouted an order as he pushed Lara toward the cubicle.

"He told you to undress and get in the shower. Don't fight him." Ricardo turned away from her and lifted his face toward the spray. "It will be over soon."

She had thought nothing could be as humiliating as what had happened in the bathroom, but it appeared she had been mistaken. Lara drew a deep breath, jerked the gauze gown over her head, and dropped it on the floor. She ran toward the shower stall, avoiding the guards' clutching hands, if not their stares and lewd remarks. She ducked beneath the cold spray and turned her back to the guards, staring desperately up at Ricardo's face. "I hate this. I hate *them*." She could feel the tears running down her cheeks and she didn't know if they were tears of anger, embarrassment, or fear. "I'd like to—"

"Shh, I know." He kept his gaze on the gray formica wall over her head as he reached for the soap. "Just think of something else."

Her gaze dropped to his chest and she inhaled sharply. Now that she was closer she could see his abdomen was crisscrossed with tiny scars. "What—"

"An ice pick. One of Jurado's less subtle methods." He began to massage the soap into her hair. "He prefers an electric cattle prod."

Lara felt sick. "I'm so sorry."

"Why? It's over."

The torture was over perhaps, but she doubted if the memory could ever leave someone who had suffered the treatment Ricardo had undergone. "I feel ashamed. I'm weeping like an idiot over having them stare at me when you—"

"Hush." His tone was as gentle as his hands massaging the soap into her hair. "It's the little humiliations that hurt the most." He made a face. "Though I'm afraid I didn't ascribe to that doctrine when Jurado was wielding the cattle prod." He tilted her head back and let the cold spray wash the soap from her hair and then turned her around so that she stood with her back to him. "You said you wanted dogs. What kind of dogs do you like?"

"Mutts. Big furry mutts. They seem to have more character." She could hear the guards laughing and she kept her gaze fixed on the wall. "I can't stand this. When can we get out of here?"

"They'll get bored soon." He added half under his breath, "Or so hot, they'll go looking for one of the *putas* who serve the prison." He pushed her forward so that he stood in the full stream of the spray. "I had a Labrador when I was a boy. He went with me everywhere."

"I've never had a pet. I meant to get one when Brett and I left our foster home, but then we were both in college and it didn't seem fair."

"What did you study in college?"

"Pre-law. I want to be a lawyer. I've always— Are they still looking at me?"

"Yes." His voice was thick. "And at me." He took a step back. "Jurado's going to be very pleased with their report."

Lara stiffened as she realized what he meant. He was aroused. "I thought cold showers were supposed to—"

"Not after five months. I feel as if I'm turning it to steam as it hits me. Lord, your skin seems to shimmer. Do you know how much I want to touch you?"

She moistened her lips with her tongue. "What was your dog's name?"

"I don't remember." His laugh held a note of desperation. "I can't remember anything."

The water didn't feel cold to her any longer either

and she was barely conscious of the gaze of the guards, she realized with amazement. Ricardo was no longer touching her, but she could sense him only inches away, and she had a mental picture of him as she had seen him just a moment ago standing beneath the spray, his long dark hair as lustrous and thick as seal fur, his lean body as tan and tough as well-oiled leather. What had they been talking about, she wondered hazily. Dogs. What a crazy thing to discuss at a time like this. "It's not good to raise big dogs in the city," she said breathlessly. "They need to run."

"We didn't live in the city. My family had a rancho at the tip of the island. You have a mole just in the hollow of your spine."

"Do I? I didn't know that."

"It's very tiny." Ricardo's voice was so soft, she could barely hear it. "Right at the exact place where your bottom starts to swell so sweetly." He was silent for an instant. "The water is polishing you, making you gleam like burnished gold."

She could feel her breasts swell as they lifted and fell with the swift acceleration of her breathing. The muscles of her stomach clenched helplessly.

Lara heard a sudden shout of laughter and then a swift barrage of Spanish from the guards. "What are they saying?"

He was silent a moment before he said hoarsely, "That you're ready for me, that I should cover you as a stallion does a mare, that I should make you spread your legs and sink deep into you. That I'm a fool to wait any longer."

Dear God, she *was* ready for him. How could such a savage, primitive response happen under circumstances like these? Her voice was muffled, strangled.

"This isn't me. I don't want this. We have to get out of here."

She could hear the harsh sound of his breathing behind her. "You're damn right we do. I'll leave first and throw on my clothes. You stay here until I call you. They'll be too busy taunting me to bother you."

She could feel a shift of air, a withdrawal of warmth, and he was gone. She closed her eyes and reached out blindly to press her palms on the wet formica-covered wall of the shower cubicle.

She tried to shut her ears to the guards' laughter, block out everything but the sound of the spray hitting the tiles.

"Lara."

She lifted her head and braced herself.

"Now, Lara."

She turned and bolted from the shower. Ricardo was standing only a few feet away, her gown in his hands. She ignored the guards by the door, her gaze clinging desperately to Ricardo's face.

He smiled at her, a smile so tender and comforting that she caught her breath. Then the gown was enveloping her, being pulled over her head and then quickly down, covering her. Not that it covered very much, she thought gloomily; her wet body caused the wet cotton gauze to cling wherever it touched.

"See, it's all right. You did fine. You were very brave, *querida*." He gently smoothed the wet hair away from her face before gathering it over her left shoulder to wring the water from its thick length. Lara felt an odd quiver of pride ripple through her at his words. She felt as if he had given her a medal. He continued softly, "It's all over now."

Was it over? Perhaps the humiliation was finished, but she felt as if something else had just begun. She had been joined, if not physically, then certainly emotionally, with Ricardo during those minutes in the shower. The experience of shared desire, shared humiliation, shared isolation, had made her dependent on him as she had never been dependent on anyone else in her life. The bond still existed. She couldn't seem to look away from him. "You shouldn't touch me, should you?" she whispered.

"No. Not like this." His hands dropped away from her hair. "Lust is all right. Tenderness . . ." He turned away abruptly. "No, I shouldn't have touched you." He held out his hand. "Come with me. Stay close and hurry." His lips tightened to a hard line. "We need to get back to the cell double quick. I don't think I could stand having them put their hands on you right now."

She slipped her hand in his, and his clasp quickly tightened around it.

Strength.

Safety.

Bonding.

The door of the cell closed behind them, shutting out the snickering remarks of the guards. The cell was dark, its only illumination the moonlight streaming through the window bars to pattern the floor as the sunlight had previously done.

She could discern Ricardo only as a shadowy silhouette as he strode across the cell to stand with his back to her at the window. He reached out with a curiously violent gesture and gripped a bar with one hand as if he wanted to rip it from the window.

"Thank you," she said quietly.

"For what?" he asked. "Not raping you in front of those guards? They haven't turned me into that kind of an animal yet."

"You were kind to me. You helped me."

"It wasn't personal. I don't care anything about you. I *can't* care anything about you."

She stood gazing at the rigid line of his spine from across the cell. As she watched, he lowered his head to rest it against the arm upraised to grip the bar. That gesture held a world of weariness and somehow touched her, hurt her. "I realize it wasn't personal, but you made that ghastly situation easier for me and—"

"Go to bed." His words were muffled against his arm.

She hesitated, uncertain what to do. She didn't want to go to bed. She wanted to go across the room and comfort him. He seemed terribly alone in this moment.

"Go on," he said.

"Where will you sleep?"

"On the floor. I'm used to it. I can sleep anywhere."

She moved slowly to the cot across the room. "You take the pillow."

He released his grip on the bar and turned to face her. "I don't want—"

"You take the pillow," she repeated stubbornly, and tossed it to him. "After the day I've had, I think I could sleep in a cactus bed."

"Don't say that too loud. Jurado will probably get rid of the cot and have one set up tomorrow."

Lara stretched out on the cot and closed her eyes. The oppressive heat of the day had vanished and the cool wind blowing into the cell sent a shiver through her. "There aren't any cactus plants on Saint Pierre, are there?"

"Jurado would have them flown in." He paused. "Why are you shivering?"

"How did you—" she stopped. The man was positively uncanny. He couldn't possibly see anything but a pale blur in the darkness, but he had detected that almost imperceptible movement. "My gown's wet. If you remember, I didn't wait to dry off."

He was silent a moment. "I remember." He was suddenly moving in the darkness. "Take it off."

"What?"

"You can't afford to get sick in this hellhole. My shirt is dry; you can wear it to sleep in tonight."

"But won't you be chilled?"

"I can close it out." He tossed her the shirt. "Wear it."

She hesitated and then sat up and slowly pulled the gown over her head. He was right; it was stupid to take a chance on becoming ill when they had so many more threats facing them. She slipped on the shirt and buttoned it to the chin. The material still held the heat of his body and smelled of soap and perspiration.

"How do you close it out?"

"There are ways. I just have to concentrate."

She laid the cotton gown on the floor and stretched out again on the cot. "Like yoga?"

"A little. Yoga, self-hypnosis. I use my own mixed bag of techniques."

So that was how he survived the torture. "Can you shut out everything?"

Another silence. "No, not everything."

The stillness of the cell was suddenly charged again. She felt the same hot, dizzy excitement she had experienced in the shower knowing he stood behind her, wanting her. Crazy. Feeling like this about Ricardo Lázaro was insane. He represented every insecurity she feared in life.

"For the Lord's sake, go to sleep."

She could hear the slight increase in the tempo of his breathing, caught the cord of tension in his voice, stretched taut, ready to break. She closed her eyes, but that was worse. Robbing herself of vision made her other senses all the more acute. It was the scent of his shirt, not the man himself, she inhaled with every breath, she told herself. He was five feet away and she couldn't possibly feel the warmth his body was exuding. "That's an excellent idea. Good night, Ricardo."

He sank to the floor beneath the window, linking his hands loosely together over his knees in the same position he had assumed earlier in the day. "*Buenas noches*, Lara."

The soft way he said her name was like dark, sensuous music. She curled up on the cot, trying to shut the thought of him out of her mind. Exquisite sensitivity and quiet, hard-edged strength. Poet-warrior.

She must not let him affect her like this, she told herself desperately. She was here for only one reason and that was to make sure he escaped from the Abbey and gave her a promise to keep Brett out of his damn war. She must not let him capture her imagination and emotions as he had her brother's. It was only being so closely confined with him, sharing this enforced intimacy, that was causing her to react in a manner so unlike her usual sensible self. She had counted on walking away from this encounter with no emotional baggage. She had not thought a bond could be forged in the short time they would have together, but she couldn't deny that something had happened between them.

She forced herself to relax her muscles and breathe deeply, steadily. All would be well. She just had to get through the next two days and she would be on her way back to the world she knew and understood.

She only had to get through the next two days.

She was still awake.

Ricardo could almost feel the waves of tension Lara emitted across the short distance separating them, and his linked hands slowly clenched together until the knuckles whitened.

She had come to help him and he was not an animal.

But, dear heaven, he wanted her.

She was little more than a child, a brave child blundering into an ugliness of which she could have no conception.

The graceful line of her spine flowing into the swelling womanliness of wet, gleaming buttocks . . .

A woman should have the right to choose her lover, and Lara had been given no choice.

She wouldn't refuse him. She might protest at first, but he was skilled enough to wake her to the realization that she wanted him as much as he wanted her.

Seduction? And where was his fine philosophy now? Seduction deprived one of free choice as surely as force.

He hurt. He wanted to touch her, to move

between her thighs and hear her cry out in a frenzy.

And Jurado would win. The bastard would have them.

Paco would attack day after tomorrow and Jurado wouldn't be sure enough of Lara's hold on him to move before the attack.

Lord, was he so depraved, he'd be willing to risk what would happen to Lara if he were wrong?

No!

His teeth bit into his lower lip until he tasted the coppery taste of blood on his tongue.

He had only to get through the next two days.

"Your lip is cut." Lara's concerned gaze lingered on Ricardo's lower lip. "I didn't notice that before."

"It's nothing." He popped the last bite of melon on his plate into his mouth. "Finish what's on your plate. You won't get anything else for the rest of the day."

"I'm not hungry." The heat in the cell was suffocating, the air as hard to breathe as it had been yesterday. Lara pushed the plate of fruit away. "Not exactly high in protein."

"It's cheaper for them to gather fruit from the rain forest. I usually get meat once a week." Ricardo took her plate and his own and set them beside the door. "It's enough."

"How do we get through today?"

"The same way I do every day." He dropped to the floor and began to do push-ups. "Exercise first."

She watched him from the cot. She still wore his shirt and she could see the flex and pull of the muscles of his arms and abdomen as he went on exercising for an incredibly long time.

"You do this every day?"

"Several times a day. Exercise pumps oxygen to the brain and makes me more alert. Lassitude is a danger in a situation like this." His tan torso gleamed with perspiration, but he was breathing only slightly heavier than when he had started. When he finally stopped, Ricardo leaned back against the wall and grinned at her. "Your turn."

"No, thank you. My idea of exercise is a swim at the YWCA every few days."

"I should have guessed you were a swimmer. Swimming muscles are smoother." His gaze focused on her calves and then traveled up to her naked thighs. "Sleeker."

The last word was thicker, huskier, than the ones that had gone before and she resisted the temptation to pull down the shirt. Instead, she jumped up and reached for the gauze gown she had laid on the floor last night. "This must be dry now. If you'll close your eyes for a minute, I'll give you back your shirt."

He obediently closed his eyes, tilting his head back against the wall. "You didn't sleep well last night."

"No." She unbuttoned the shirt and let it slide down her arms. "How did you know?"

"I didn't sleep well either."

She pulled the gown over her head and settled it over her hips. "You said it wouldn't bother you to sleep on the floor."

"It seems I was wrong."

"You can open your eyes now."

His lids flicked open and he smiled at her. "I think I like you in my shirt better."

She avoided his eyes as she picked up the shirt and tossed it to him. "Neither of us has a large wardrobe here. You can't afford to give me your clothes." She sat down on the cot and raised her arms and began to run her fingers through her hair, trying to comb out the tangles. "I don't suppose you have a brush?"

He shook his head.

"I didn't think so." She made a face. "It's funny how we take things like brushes for granted and never realize how—" She broke off as she looked up to see him watching her. "Why are you looking at me like that?"

"Like what?" He pulled his gaze away and shifted it to the floor. "I was just looking."

She glanced down at herself and suddenly realized her raised arms had pulled the bodice of the gown taut, revealing the shadowy outline of her nipples pressed against the gauze. She hurriedly lowered her arms and searched desperately for something to break the silence. "Aren't you going to put on your shirt?"

"Not yet." He slowly raised his gaze to meet her own. "It still has your scent."

A wave of heat tingled through her, and the breath left her body.

He glanced away again, one hand clenching the material of the shirt. "Why don't we play word games?"

What else had they been playing? she wondered wildly. "Word games?"

He sat up straighter. "It will give us something to do. Take our minds off . . . " His brow furrowed in a frown. "Twenty Questions. We'll play Twenty

Questions. I'm thinking of something. Try to guess what it is."

She hoped it wasn't what she was thinking about.

His frown vanished and his sudden smile held a hint of mischief. He pursed his lips reprovingly and silently shook his head.

Drat the man, it was clear he had guessed exactly what her thoughts had been. Still, the amusement had lightened the atmosphere between them and that change was certainly welcome.

She sat down on the cot and smiled back at him. "Is what you're thinking about animal, vegetable, or mineral?"

Three

_____

"You cheated." Lara sat back on her heels and glared accusingly at Ricardo. "Everyone thinks of a whale as a fish."

"It's a mammal," Ricardo said with a complacent smile. "You didn't ask the right questions. Don't blame me if you think of a whale as a fish. What the devil did they teach you in that college?"

"A whale swims in the sea. Why shouldn't I think of—" She stopped and broke out laughing. "Boy, was that a dumb mistake. All right, you got me."

"It's about time you admitted it. I've never seen a woman as stubborn as you are."

She wrinkled her nose at him. "I don't like to lose."

"Obviously." He gazed at her thoughtfully. "And you don't lose often. You're very bright. I think we broke about even for the day."

Lara nodded. "But I would have tipped the scales my way if you hadn't come up with that blasted whale."

The rays of the sun streaming through the window onto the stone floor had lengthened and she noticed in surprise that it must be late afternoon. The hours had flown by at light speed while they had played a variety of word games before finally returning to Twenty Questions. She had become so involved, she had almost forgotten where she was and the danger surrounding them.

Ricardo had made her forget. In the past hours he had shown her another side of his character entirely. His wit had made her laugh, his cleverness had aroused her admiration, and his zestful enthusiasm had swept her up and away from their depressing surroundings like a runaway roller coaster.

"How do you do it?" she asked suddenly, her laughter fading. "How do you manage not to let being here bother you? I've only been in this cell one day and it would have driven me crazy if you hadn't taken my mind off being here."

"There are usually small pleasures you can find to distract yourself in any situation. If I hadn't been here to show you the way, you would have eventually found it yourself."

"I'm not sure you're right about that."

"I'm sure."

"Why?"

A sudden brilliant smile lit his face. "Because you don't like to lose."

She chuckled. "I can't deny that, can I? But it's not the kind of—" She broke off as she heard the sound of footsteps coming down the hallway. She tensed, her gaze flying to the door.

"Easy," Ricardo said quietly, sitting up straighter. "It could be nothing."

"Or something." She moistened her lips with her tongue. "Animal, vegetable, or mineral?"

"Good." Ricardo's tone reflected both surprise and respect. "Laughter will always keep you from losing, Lara."

A key was being inserted in the lock.

"I'll try to remember that. Though it's going to be—" She broke off as the door was thrown open and Jurado strode into the cell followed by two guards.

"Animal," Ricardo said precisely. "No guessing there."

Lara found herself laughing even as she felt fear tighten her throat.

"Very amusing," Jurado said as he looked at both of them. "Evidently your entire day has been amusing."

"If you didn't want us to have fun, you should have joined us instead of eavesdropping." Ricardo stretched his legs, crossing them at the ankle. "The sight of you usually succeeds in putting a damper on any party."

"I didn't put the woman here for you to play children's games with her." Jurado's voice held barely restrained fury. "You sounded like two squabbling infants."

"Sorry." Ricardo shrugged. "Maybe I think of her as an infant. You'll just have to wait and see if I change my mind, won't you?"

"Will I?" Jurado crossed the cell in two strides and grabbed Lara's wrist. "I don't like to wait." He jerked her to her feet. "You didn't think of her as an infant last night in the shower. My guards have eyes."

Ricardo stiffened as his gaze shifted to Lara's

frightened face. "You're angry with me, not her. Let her go."

"Oh, no. I think you need a little jolt to make you realize who is in control here." He pulled Lara toward the door. "My guards don't think of her as an infant."

"No!" Ricardo jumped to his feet. His expression was guarded, but his muscles were bunched as if ready to spring. Then his stance changed as he forced himself to relax. "All right, I admit I find her desirable. Is that enough for you, Jurado?"

"Of course not. She still goes with me."

Terror iced through Lara as Jurado jerked her toward the door. She would not cry, she told herself fiercely. This entire scenario was aimed at Ricardo and she knew Jurado wanted her to weep and plead to make it more difficult for him.

"Do you want me to beg?" Ricardo asked hoarsely. "Very well, I'll do it. She has nothing to do with our war. Don't hurt her, Jurado."

"No please?" Jurado taunted as he glanced at Ricardo over his shoulder.

"Please," Ricardo grated, through clenched teeth.

"It's not enough. I believe I'll let you have time alone to consider how much you appreciate the woman's company."

"What are you going to do to her?"

"I'll let you guess." Jurado's eyes gleamed with malicious enjoyment. "You know me. What do you think I'll do to her?"

"Jurado, damn you. Don't do—"

The slamming of the door of the cell cut off Ricardo's protest, and Jurado propelled Lara down the corridor toward the door of the cell block.

* * *

The last rays of the setting sun were streaming into the cell when Jurado returned Lara over three hours later.

Ricardo's gaze flew to Lara's face, but Jurado gave her no time to speak as he pushed her across the cell toward Ricardo. "Did you miss her, Lázaro?"

Ricardo's gaze never left Lara's face. "What did they do to you?"

"Now, does she look ill treated?" Jurado pushed Lara to her knees on the stone floor before Ricardo. "We thought we'd made her quite attractive." He touched a silky strand of Lara's fair hair. "She's showered and perfumed, and we even brushed her hair until it shone. She couldn't have had a more personal beauty treatment at the most exclusive salon in the United States. And all for you, Lázaro."

"Is that what they did to you?" Ricardo's gaze searched her expression. "*Tell* me, Lara."

She nodded. "It was enough." A shudder went through her. "Their hands on me. I hated it."

Jurado leisurely began to undo the buttons at the bodice of Lara's gauze gown. "She's most unappreciative. She doesn't realize how lenient I've been to her, does she, Lázaro?" He pushed back the folds of material to reveal the upper slopes of Lara's breasts. "But you realize how much worse it could have been." He said softly, "Doesn't she have pretty breasts? Don't you want to touch them?"

"No."

"I think you do." Jurado smiled. "If you don't touch them, I will. Do you want to see me fondle her?"

"I'm going to kill you one day, Jurado."

"How fierce you are." His smile faded. "Touch her, Lázaro."

Ricardo stood unmoving, looking down at Lara.

Jurado's voice cracked whiplike in the room. "Touch her. Fondle her."

Ricardo dropped to his knees in front of Lara. "I'm sorry," he whispered. "Lord, I'm sorry."

"I know you are." Her eyes were bright with tears. "It's all right."

His gaze held her own as his hands slowly slipped into the opening of her gown and gently cupped her breasts.

She closed her eyes and drew a shaky breath as his warm, callused palms caressed her. She had expected to feel defiled, but there was nothing crude or obscene about Ricardo's touch, only the most exquisite tenderness.

"I see you like her," Jurado said with satisfaction. "I knew you would."

"Shut up, Jurado." Ricardo's voice was thick. "You're getting what you want."

"Not entirely. She looks like a sensual angel kneeling there with her hair flowing about her. How could any man resist taking her to bed? I really believe I've outdone myself."

"Get out of here and let her alone. Haven't you put her through enough?"

"You'll have your privacy soon enough. Doesn't she smell sweet?"

"Yes," Ricardo said hoarsely.

"Her breasts are really quite lovely. How does it feel to have your hands on her?"

Ricardo didn't answer.

"You don't have to answer. I can see for myself. These five months are telling on you, Lázaro." Lara heard the sound of footsteps as Jurado crossed the cell. "I'm leaving you now. Do enjoy yourselves." He paused at the door. "And you *will* enjoy her tonight, Lázaro. Matters aren't proceeding quickly enough to suit me. I'll give you until midnight. If you don't perform with suitable virility and enthusiasm, I'll take her to the guards' quarters."

Lara's eyes opened as the door slammed behind Jurado. Ricardo's olive complexion was paler than she had ever seen it and lines of strain carved either side of his mouth.

"Are you really all right?" he asked thickly.

She nodded jerkily. "It wasn't pleasant, but perhaps Jurado's right and I should feel lucky." She looked down at his hands still covering her breasts. A tingling shock went through her as she saw the contrast of tan hardness against her softer fairness. The hot color rose to her cheeks as she felt her nipples harden against his palms in mindless response.

His gaze followed her own and he stared for an instant as if mesmerized before he drew a deep, harsh breath and slowly withdrew his hands from beneath her gown.

Her breasts felt chilled without his warmth. She said hurriedly, "Thank you for trying to keep them from taking me. It couldn't have been easy for you to plead with that bastard."

"Pride doesn't mean much when—" He broke off and began to button her gown. "I'd have done a hell of a lot more to keep them from putting you through that."

His fingers were trembling and her concerned gaze lifted to his face. "I'm really fine. You don't need to worry."

"Worry?" His voice was shaking as his hand

reached out to cup her cheek. "Do you know what I felt waiting here helplessly while I imagined what they were doing to you?"

She glanced anxiously at the microphone on the wall. "Be careful. Jurado should be back in his office at any moment."

"We still have a minute or two. Don't you see? It's too late, damn his soul," he laughed harshly. "He has us."

She nodded. "I know he has us."

"And a big part of me is happy as hell I get to take what I want." His tone was tormented. "What kind of man does that make me?"

"Human." She tried to keep her voice even. "It's all right, Ricardo. I knew this might happen when I came here."

"Did you?" His expression was agonized as he leaned forward and whispered into her hair, "We have to stall him until after tomorrow morning. Sex is nothing to Jurado and it's hard for him to believe it can mean anything to someone else. He should give me a few days to become attached to you after . . ." He smoothed her hair back from her face. "But he'll prey on anything softer, so we have to be very careful. You understand?"

"I understand." But Ricardo didn't understand, she thought with a shiver of apprehension, and how would he react when he did? She sat back on her heels and looked up at him. "Well, we don't seem to have many options, do we?"

He slowly shook his head. "Jurado's not bluffing. He gave me those three hours of hell to make sure I knew I wouldn't have another chance."

Her stare dropped to the middle button of his shirt. "Then I guess we'll have to do what he wants."

Ricardo muttered a curse under his breath.

The color flew to her cheeks. "If you can. Being ordered to make love to a woman must be a complete turnoff."

"Oh, I can." Ricardo laughed shortly. "Believe me, I can. I'm so hot, I could have taken you in front of Jurado, and the bastard knew it."

And she had known it too. Even with her eyes closed she had felt his hunger and need as he had fondled her breasts.

His need and her own.

"Then it will be easy for you to—"

"But it won't be easy for you." Ricardo interrupted harshly. "Dammit, you're a virgin. Suppose I hurt you?"

She smiled tremulously. "I don't think you'd hurt me as much as Jurado's guards."

"A great choice," Ricardo muttered. "Lord, this shouldn't be happening to you. Why can't I *do* something?"

She could sense his torment as she had his need and she felt an overpowering desire to rid him of it. "Stop torturing yourself," she said lightly. "You're not destroying my life. Virginity is nothing in this day and age. I've just been too busy to rid myself of it."

"It's not 'nothing' to the man who—" Ricardo broke off and drew a deep breath. "I'll try to make it easy for you."

Her gaze lifted to his face. "Now?"

He shook his head. "There's no hurry. We have until midnight and I refuse to perform on demand. We'll find a way not to lose to Jurado." A sudden smile lit his face. "You must make me a promise. I want you to forget about the microphone and Jurado and where we are."

She looked at him in bewilderment. "How can I do that?"

"Concentrate. You forgot them all for a while earlier today when we were playing games." His smile faded and his intent gaze met her own. "I won't have you remember this as a horror." His voice lowered. "Do this for me, *por favor.*"

She couldn't look away from him. He was suddenly different from the quiet, self-disciplined man she had known since she had walked into this cell. It was as if he had unhooded a light he had kept carefully veiled. This was the man who dominated hundreds of thousands of followers with the sheer charisma of his personality. She felt enveloped, surrounded by the force field of his will. "What do you want me to do?"

"Imagine."

The last light filtering through the bars cast a rose-gold glow over the cell, softening the barren starkness wherever it touched and leaving the rest of the cell in shadows. Ricardo's features were lit in the same ambivalent manner, his high cheekbones darkly hollowed, but the beautifully shaped lips and sparkling black eyes appeared softer, more tender. Lord, he was beautiful. "Imagine what?"

"That I'm your lover." He reached out and gently brushed a strand of hair back from her forehead. "And that there's no war, no revolution. It's a world where the only problems are fierce fathers who protect their beautiful daughters from the young men who wish to snatch them away from them." He leaned forward and his lips brushed the tip of her nose. "Go sit on the cot, *querida.*"

She rose to her feet and moved dreamily toward the cot. The golden haze didn't reach to this shadowy corner of the cell and she knew she must be only a pale blur to Ricardo. She knelt on the cot, her gaze flying back to where he was kneeling in the pool of light. "And did you snatch me away from my fierce father?"

He nodded. "From the moment I saw you, I knew I had to have you. Your father owns the rancho next to my own and every day I'd see you riding your palomino mare, your fair hair shining in the sunlight. For the last week I've watched you ride out from your father's *casa* with its red-tiled roof and high stucco walls and waited to catch a glimpse of you as you galloped by the lake that borders my property." His voice lowered. "I knew I should court you properly, but this afternoon you reined in your horse by the lake and looked at me, and I forgot everything. I think you forgot everything too."

"Yes," she whispered. "I'd never felt like that before."

"How did you feel, *querida*?"

She was silent.

"Tell me. Pretend. Imagine . . ."

She was suddenly afraid to let herself fall deeper into this make-believe that was becoming more real than the cell around her. Yet her answer came haltingly, tentatively, drawn from her by the sheer power of his personality. "As if you were a part of me that I'd never been aware existed before."

"Then it was right that I bribed your servant to smuggle me into your bedroom tonight."

"Is that where we are?"

"You must be as love struck as I am." Ricardo's tone was gently chiding. "Don't you recognize the ornamental bars your father placed on the windows to keep out suitors? The leaf-green and ivory Aubusson carpet I'm sitting on?"

She could almost see them, she realized dreamily. "But why are you sitting on the floor?"

"Where else would a suitor sit but at the feet of his lady?" His voice deepened. "Besides, I dare not touch you yet."

"Why not?"

"I must make sure that you want me as much as I want you." He began to unbutton his shirt. "You don't know the ways of passion yet and I must be careful not to hurt you."

"Yet you sneak into my father's house to take my virtue?"

"As Romeo did with Juliet. Your father thinks I'm too wild for his gentle daughter."

"Are you?"

He stripped off his shirt, and his powerful shoulders gleamed golden in the twilight. "Yes."

She inhaled sharply as she looked at him. Ricardo's glossy black hair flowed about his shoulders, and his muscles were taut, sinewy with power. He looked wild and untamed, totally different from the controlled man she had come to know. "Then why should I let you seduce me?"

He stood up, his fingers unfastening his trousers. "Because you're not the gentle girl your father thinks you are, that you think you are."

"I should know myself."

He was quickly stripping. "Then why aren't you shocked that I'm undressing in front of you?" He turned to face her, his nude body bathed in the influx of light that cast an aura of diffused gold around him. "Do you find me pleasing, Lara?"

"Yes." She cleared her throat to rid it of its tightness. Her breasts swelled beneath the gauze of her gown as she remembered the feel of Ricardo's callused palms as he had caressed her.

"Do you want to know how I find you?" He stood unmoving in the pool of light. "But I think you do know. Just as you knew this afternoon when I pulled you down off your horse in the tall grass and rubbed against you like an animal in need. I can still hear those soft, keening sounds you made deep in your throat."

"I don't remember doing that."

"Then I'll have to remind you." He moved forward to stand before her. "You kept saying, 'Ricardo, *querido*. I love you.' You arched up against me and our hands were all over each other. I wanted to take you then and there."

She felt the muscles of her stomach clench helplessly and a liquid burning between her thighs. "Why didn't you?"

His fingertips touched her cheek and she felt as if that gentle touch was burning her. "Because you're my lady and not my whore. You must have satin sheets and a chamber scented with lilac and lavender. I would have taken you to my own rancho, but you were frightened of what your father would do. So I came to you." His hand moved down to cup her throat. "As I'll always come to you."

She gazed up at him, mesmerized. Dear heaven, she could actually smell the lilac and lavender, she thought helplessly. And this was her lover who had risked everything so that she might have a night to remember. She whispered, "Why?"

"Because we were meant to be together." His hand slipped into the opening of her gown and it trembled as it had before. "You belong to me." His thumbnail brushed against her nipple, and a streak of fire surged through her. "And I belong to you."

He withdrew his hand and reached down to kiss her softly, sweetly, lingeringly. "Let's get rid of the gown, Lara. Lovers shouldn't have barriers between them, should they?"

"No." She knelt in a dreamy haze as he pulled the gown over her head and dropped it on the floor. The light was fading and the shadows were merging and becoming darkness as Ricardo pushed her gently back on the cot and moved over her, parting her thighs, cupping her womanhood with one warm hand as he bent and kissed her again.

His tongue invaded her mouth as his hand began to rub, explore in its own sensual invasion.

She moaned deep in her throat as she had in the tall grass when he had first touched her.

He lifted his head and smiled down at her. "Yes, that's my wild love." His fingers plunged deep and she arched up toward him with a cry. His breathing harshened. "*Want* me, Lara."

She did want him. She was on fire. Her teeth sank into her lower lip to smother the cries that kept welling from her throat as he stroked, rotated. It was as if a dam had burst and everything inside her was flowing toward him in a hot tide. "Ricardo, it's—" She stopped, panting as he moved over her. "Yes. Yes."

"Now?" He whispered, "I may hurt you, *querida*. Your father is right. I'm too wild for you."

"No, you're not." Her hands clutched his shoulders, afraid he'd leave her. "I need you, Ricardo."

"Do you?" He slowly lowered his head until his

lips were hovering only a breath above her own. "Then take me, Lara."

He plunged deep and her cry was muffled by his lips. He stopped, his manhood within her, his lips pressed to her own, letting her get used to him.

The sensation was indescribable. Fullness, heat, hunger.

He raised his head and looked down at her. His chest lifted and fell with the harshness of his breathing, and his features were contorted with pleasure. "If I'm hurting you, you'll have to tell me to stop. I can't do it on my own."

She shook her head. She couldn't force the words past her lips.

He drew a deep breath that she felt within her own body. Then he was moving, plunging, thrusting with the wildness he had warned her might be loosed.

She welcomed the storm, her head thrashing back and forth on the sheet as his hands slid beneath her buttocks, lifting her into each thrust.

She knew she was moaning, whimpering, but she couldn't stop. She couldn't do anything but respond to the fiery rhythm he had set. She felt taken, absorbed, possessed, and yet she still wanted to give more.

"Now, *querida*," he whispered against her mouth. "Let it happen."

She closed her eyes as the rhythm escalated. Tall, fragrant grass, satin sheets, lilac and lavender, her lover coming to her in the darkness.

Her lover . . .

She lurched upward as the tension broke, shattering into a million shards of sensation.

"Ricardo!"

A guttural groan tore from him as his body convulsed and shudder after shudder racked through him. He collapsed against her, his heart thundering, his breath coming in gasps.

He was shaking and her arms instinctively closed maternally about him as he buried his face in her shoulder.

Her lover . . .

"It's all right," she murmured. "It's all right, now."

"Is it?" His muffled voice held a thread of desperation. "Then why can't I get the hell off you? I want to stay here and . . ." He flexed within her with mindless hunger. "Dear heaven, but I want to stay here. This is what I've wanted from the minute I saw you."

"When I was riding the palomino," she said dreamily. No, that wasn't right, that had only been Ricardo's beautiful fantasy he had painted for her. She laughed huskily. "Do you know, I almost believed it?"

"So did I." His hand smoothed her hair back from her temple. "Was it good for you, *querida*?"

"Yes. More than good. Beautiful."

He bent forward. "Then may I show you more?" He kissed her shoulder. "I can't seem to get enough of you. I'll make you want it, I promise you."

She already wanted him again, she realized with surprise. Maybe she was as wild as he had called her. No, that was the woman of the fantasy—a woman who lived in a *casa* with a red-tiled roof on a rancho with a clear blue lake and tall green grass waving in the breeze.

But the tingling heat flowing through her now was no fantasy. Her arms tightened around Ricardo's shoulders as her legs wrapped around his hips. "Come to me," she whispered. "Show me."

Jurado and the guards came for her at midnight, giving her only time to draw on her gown before the guards pushed her toward the door.

Ricardo leapt from the cot. "Damn you, Jurado, you said you—"

"Compose yourself, Lázaro," Jurado interrupted. "She won't be hurt . . . yet. I quite enjoyed your little charade and I'm very pleased with you. However, I'm sure it will take a few more days to bring you to the point of no return. We just have to make sure you both weren't playacting for my benefit as well as the woman's. We have to examine her."

"For God's sake, you don't have to put her through that. She isn't—"

The slam of the door cut off his words and Ricardo was alone in the cell.

She would be frightened.

The thought made the bile rise in his throat. He couldn't stand the thought of her alone and frightened with those greasy pigs touching her.

He wanted to kill someone.

He moved to the window and watched Lara walk across the courtyard toward the infirmary between the two guards.

Agony tore through him and he could feel the hot tears sting his eyes.

Lara flew across the room toward him as soon as the cell door slammed behind her.

"I want to go back." Tears ran down her cheeks as she came into his arms. "Ricardo . . ."

He held her close. "Lord, you're cold."

"I feel cold. I feel as if I'll never get warm. The table was metal and there was a bare bulb burning above me." The words tumbled feverishly as her arms closed fiercely around him. "It was ugly. Uglier than it was before."

"Shh, I know."

"Everything was ugly. I felt as if I couldn't breathe without inhaling filth. I want to go back."

He picked her up as if she were a small child and carried her toward the cot. She was shaking as if with a chill. "Back home to the United States?"

"No." Her eyes closed as she nestled closer to him. "Why should I want to go there? I want to go back to the rancho."

He stopped in midstride, looking down at her. She was almost in shock and who could blame her after all that had happened to her? "You can't go—" He stopped. She had faced enough ugly reality for one day; a little fantasy could do her no harm. He sat down on the cot and held her on his lap, rocking her back and forth. "We *are* back at the rancho, Lara."

She felt light and womanly in his arms and for an instant he felt a familiar stirring in his groin. No, not now. The last thing Lara needed now was sex. She only wanted escape from this sordidness. She wanted the feeling that she was safe and free.

"The tall grass by the lake," she murmured, as if prompting him.

"We tied our horses to the cypress tree." He stroked her hair gently. "You brought a picnic basket today and you're laughing and telling me not to spread the red-checkered tablecloth on the anthill. There are water lilies floating on the lake and my Labrador is racing along the bank chasing a squirrel."

"I remember the Labrador. You never told me his name."

"Jaime." His lips pressed against her temple and he felt the tenderness well up in him. "His name is Jaime and he loves you very much."

"Does he?" She cuddled closer. She was silent a moment before whispering, "You must think I'm crazy. I know it's not true, Ricardo. I just want it to be true for a little while. I *need* it to be true."

"Then it is true. It's all true. Close your eyes and you'll see it." His palm passed over her lids, closing them. "The sun is shining on your face and it's making you drowsy. I'll spread a blanket on the ground so you can nap before we go back to the rancho."

"My father will catch us if you take me back."

"No, have you forgotten? Our rancho. We're married now. Two weeks ago, in the chapel in the village. You belong to me."

Lara woke slowly, peacefully, her lids opening to see Ricardo's face above her. He smiled. "Good morning."

"Good morning."

Sunlight streamed into the cell, touching his black hair with vibrant luster. How odd that she should feel this supreme contentment as she looked at him. It was as if they'd awakened together like this a thousand times before. "What time is it?"

Ricardo glanced at the sun streaming through the bars. "I'd judge it to be close to eight."

Eight o'clock. After the shocks she'd undergone last night, she hadn't expected to sleep this late. There wasn't much time.

Lara quickly sat up and swung her feet to the floor as she ran her fingers nervously through her hair. Lord, she was frightened. What if something went wrong?

"What's the matter?" Ricardo's gaze narrowed on her face.

"What could be the matter?" she said softly. "You love me."

Ricardo darted a glance at the microphone on the wall. "That was only pretense, Lara."

"No." Her tone was urgent. "I know you love me. How many times did you whisper it to me last night?"

"Lara, what the hell are you doing?"

"If you love me, you can't let them hurt me." Her voice rose hysterically. "You have to tell them what you know. You can't let them touch me again. None of this is my fault."

Ricardo sat up, his face suddenly pale. "I said nothing to you last night that couldn't be said to a child I wished to comfort."

"You lie." Her voice was shrill. "Why are you lying to me? You said it was a secret between us that you loved me, that you would always love me. I don't want them to hurt me. Tell them."

Ricardo's gaze desperately shifted to the microphone again. "I'm not lying. You were a good lay and I needed a woman. You mean nothing to me. Nothing."

"Ricardo." She tried to make her voice quaver.

She didn't have to try very hard; she was shivering as if with a chill. "I've made you angry. Don't be angry with me. Just tell them what they want to know so they'll let me go."

Ricardo jumped to his feet and strode toward the window and looked out into the courtyard. He muttered a low curse. "Jurado's coming. Mother of God, he's *coming*. What the hell have you done?"

Lara sat back on the cot, trying to subdue the fear clutching at her. The plan had been put into motion and it was too late for regrets now. "What I had to do."

Ricardo ran across the room and sent the microphone crashing to the floor before turning to face her. "Damn you, what the hell do you mean by all this?"

She met his gaze and answered quietly, "I didn't want to lose and this was the only way to win. You were right. Renalto couldn't have freed you from this cell block, but the interrogation room adjoins Jurado's office. He can get to you there and run no danger from the machine gun on the roof. He said it was the only way."

He gazed at her in disbelief. "My Lord, do you know what they'll do to you?"

"There won't be time. Renalto should be here any moment."

"Damn you, why didn't you tell me what you were planning?"

"Renalto said you wouldn't let—"

The cell door was unlocked and thrown open.

Lara quickly closed her eyes and began making low, whimpering noises in her throat.

"She's not a fit mate for you, Lázaro," Jurado said

in disgust. "She's too weak. Look at her, moaning and hysterical, and we've scarcely touched her."

"You're right," Ricardo said quickly. "She's nothing to me, less than nothing."

"Perhaps," Jurado said. "But we all know your weakness for the helpless. Maybe you do care something for her. I think we'll see if we can spark a response." He moved across the room and grabbed Lara's hair and jerked back her head. "Stop that moaning; it annoys me."

She opened her eyes to see Jurado's round, boyish face above her. "Please, don't hurt me. Don't let them touch me again, Ricardo."

"No courage." Jurado's lips curled in disgust as he released her hair, turned, and strode from the cell. "Bring them both. We'll try the whip first, I think."

Lara's glance flew to Ricardo.

He wasn't looking at her, and his expression was flint hard as the guards pushed him toward the door.

The lash struck Lara's back, tearing through the cotton gauze of her gown.

Her spine arched and she strained against the leather manacles holding her upright. Was it the fifth or sixth blow?

"Well, Lázaro?"

Ricardo's tone was expressionless. "Do what you wish. She means nothing to me."

The whip struck again, harder.

Where was Renalto?

The whip struck again.

"She means nothing to me."

How many times had he said those words? They seemed to be burning into her back with every searing stroke of the whip.

She couldn't see any longer. The tears ran down her cheeks, blurring everything in the room.

"You might as well stop. Why should I speak? She's just a woman who pleased me for a few hours."

The whip struck again.

Her flesh was growing numb. Perhaps it wouldn't hurt at all soon.

The room was growing darker.

The chatter of a machine gun . . .

Shouts.

Did they really exist or had she imagined it?

Jurado was screaming orders.

Someone was freeing her from the leather manacles.

He shouldn't have done that, she thought hazily. Didn't he know she couldn't stand alone?

Her legs buckled and she fell to her knees on the floor.

"Lara . . ."

It was Ricardo's voice, but he sounded hoarse, strange.

She tried to lift her head to see his face.

It was too difficult; her neck felt odd, like a fragile stem that would snap if she tried to move it.

It didn't matter. She probably couldn't have seen him anyway. Everything was growing so dark.

She pitched forward as the darkness overwhelmed her.

Four
_____

Stalactites.

Beige-, peach-, and cream-colored stalactites hung down from the high ceiling above her like giant jagged icicles.

"It must be quite a shock waking up to this. You're in the caverns."

Her glance flickered to Paco Renalto's face. She was lying on a pallet on a stone floor, she realized, and Renalto sat cross-legged on the floor beside her.

"The caverns?" She looked around her in bewilderment. She appeared to be in a small chamber of some sort, if you could call a naturally formed room in a cave a chamber. Three lanterns affixed to the craggy walls burned brightly in a valiant attempt to dispel the darkness. The room contained no furniture or comforts other than the pallet on which she was lying. She knew there was something she should remember about the caverns. . . . It was the password Renalto had given her to identify herself to Ricardo at the Abbey! Suddenly everything flowed back to her with overwhelming force. Ricardo, the Abbey, the lash striking her back.

"The caverns network these hills and we use them as an arms cache and primary base of operations," Paco said quickly, his concerned gaze on her suddenly shadowed face. "How do you feel?"

"Lousy," she whispered. "Ricardo?"

"Safe. He carried you here."

"You were . . . late."

"I know." He grimaced and the expression made his puckish features look more elfin than before. "It took longer than we had thought to get rid of the perimeter guards and cut off the voltage of the fence. I'm sorry, Lara."

She tried to smile. "I suppose it couldn't be helped."

"You're more generous than Ricardo. He raved at me like a maniac. You were very brave, *pequeña*."

She shook her head. "I was scared to death."

"But Ricardo said you never cried out once while Jurado was having you whipped."

"Why should I give him that satisfaction? I knew he wouldn't stop, and it would have made it harder for Ricardo and me too." She shifted and flinched as hot pain flashed through her back. "How badly did he hurt me?"

"There will be no permanent scarring, but you'll be uncomfortable for a few days. Ricardo had the doctor dress and bandage your back as soon as we reached the caverns."

"Jurado?"

"Still alive, unfortunately," he said regretfully. "He slipped out of the interrogation room when we attacked and we had no time to search for him. We thought it best to get you and Ricardo safely away before reinforcements arrived from the cell block."

"When can I get up?"

"As soon as you feel well enough."

Lara carefully levered herself up on one elbow. Another hot flash of pain shivered down her spine and her head began to swim. "I think . . . I'll wait awhile."

"I thought you would." Paco picked up a tin cup from the ground beside him. "Drink this."

She took the cup and looked dubiously at the milky liquid it contained. "What is it?"

"Just a sleeping powder. It works very quickly and when you wake, you'll feel much better."

"I'll drink to that." She lifted the cup and drained it. The liquid possessed a vague fruity flavor that was not unpleasant. She handed him the cup and carefully turned over on her stomach as she lay back down. "Where's Ricardo?"

"In the war room planning the campaign."

She smothered a yawn with her hand. "Already?"

"It could be the last campaign of the war. We've only been waiting for Ricardo to lead us."

More war, more violence, and Ricardo in the thick of it. She felt a cold sickness in the pit of her stomach. Hadn't he been through enough for his glorious revolution? A sudden memory of Ricardo's expression as Jurado had taken them both from the cell block came back to her. "He's angry with me."

"Yes, he's angry with both of us. I told you he would be." Paco stood up and looked down at her. "But you did well, Lara."

"Did I?" Her eyes were irresistibly closing as sleep once again claimed her. "It was all like a bad dream. I felt so helpless. . . ."

* * *

When Lara awoke some time later, she was alone and had no idea how long she had slept. The flames of the lanterns fastened to the craggy stone walls still burned brightly, but she had slept so soundly, she knew she wouldn't have awakened if someone had come in a dozen times to refill them.

She sat up slowly, gingerly, and experienced a rush of relief. Movement was still painful but at least tolerable now. She tossed aside the blanket and started to stand up.

"Wait, I'll help you."

A curly-haired boy of eight or nine appeared in the arched opening across the chamber and hurried toward her. He was dressed in the same green army fatigues as the other soldiers she had seen, but they swamped his small body. His brow was wrinkled with concern as he took her arm and helped her to her feet. "You mustn't move too quickly or you'll open the wounds, and Ricardo will be angry with me."

"Who are you?"

"I'm Manuel Delguero. I take care of you."

The words were spoken with such quaint gravity, she found herself smiling at him. "Oh, you do?"

He nodded. "It's a great honor. Ricardo said that someday the people of Saint Pierre will tell tales around the camp fires of how bravely you came to the Abbey to rescue him."

She blinked. "Somehow I doubt that."

He frowned fiercely. "Ricardo said so."

And evidently what Ricardo said was law to the boy. "What are you doing here?"

"I told you; I take care of you."

"No, I mean here in the caverns. Where are your parents?"

"Dead." His voice was without inflection. "Everyone is dead. The junta's army killed them and Ricardo brought me to the caverns to live."

"I'm sorry."

"Oh, I don't remember them. I was only a baby."

He was little more than a baby now, Lara thought with compassion. "And you live here in the caverns?"

He nodded. "For a while I lived with María in a nearby village, but three years ago Ricardo sent Paco to bring us here. María helps the doctor." His voice was proud. "And I help Ricardo. He said he needed me at his side."

The children following the Pied Piper, she thought with a bittersweet pang. "But didn't you like living in the village more than here?"

He gazed at her in bewilderment. "I'm a soldier. The revolution needed me. Ricardo needed me."

"I see." She didn't see. She didn't understand a world where young men like Brett ended up in wheelchairs and small children became soldiers. "Well, I need you to help me too. I'm filthy and this gown I'm wearing is in rags. Is there somewhere I can take a bath and then get something clean to wear?"

He nodded eagerly. "That's why I'm here. To guard you and see to your needs."

She grimaced. "Well, at least he doesn't make you carry a gun." She moved toward him, the rough stone floor cold beneath her bare feet. "Shoes. Can you find me some shoes?"

"Leave everything to me, señorita." He waved his hand grandly. "I won't fail you."

He didn't fail her. The underground pool he led

her to was icy cold but clear as a diamond. He helped her remove the bandages, provided her with shampoo, soap, towels, and a washcloth, and then discreetly turned his back as she bathed. When she came out of the water, she found he had set out green army fatigue trousers, two pairs of socks, boots, and a shirt that were all spotlessly clean. She supposed it was too much to hope for underclothing. The clothes hung almost as loosely on her small frame as Manuel's garments did on him. She rolled up the sleeves of the shirt and put on one pair of dark-gray socks and stuffed the combat boots with the other pair to make them fit.

"You shouldn't have put on the shirt." Manuel frowned in disapproval as he turned around to look at her. "Ricardo told me he wanted to look at your wounds."

"There's no need. They're healing well."

"Ricardo said he wants to look at them." Manuel's jaw set stubbornly. "I'll go get him."

"He's probably forgotten he told you that," Lara said lightly. "He has a war to run."

"Ricardo doesn't forget."

"Everyone forgets things when they're under pressure."

Manuel shook his head. "Not Ricardo." He turned on his heel and trotted off.

Another worshiper at the altar, Lara thought wearily as she began to run the brush through her damp hair. How did the man do it?

The question was rhetorical. She knew exactly how he did it. She had a taste of that charisma herself at the Abbey. With the sheer force of his personality and his honeyed tongue he had built a world that had swept her away from fear and desolation into a country where only beauty and love existed. A man with power and eloquence on such a scale could move hearts as well as mountains.

But the country he had created for her had not really existed. Those hours they spent together had been a mirage, a time apart. They had been forced together in the most intimate of circumstances, which had distorted the reality of how different they were. Now that they were free of the prison, she was sure she would be able to look at him with the same objectivity she had before she arrived on Saint Pierre. The sense of loneliness and depʲetion she had felt when she had first awakened was a bizarre aftereffect of the traumatic events at the Abbey.

"How are you?" Ricardo asked from behind her.

The brush running through her hair stopped in mid motion as her heart gave a leap. She drew a deep breath and didn't turn around as she resumed brushing her hair. "I told Manuel I was fine. You didn't need to come and see for yourself."

"But I've not always found you entirely honest."

"I've never lied to you."

"You don't always have to lie to deceive." His tone was hard and unrelenting. "You manipulated me. Paco knew I'd never permit you to put yourself into that kind of danger to save my neck."

"Things went wrong. He was supposed to arrive with the cavalry earlier," she said lightly. "I probably wouldn't have been hurt at all if everything had gone as planned."

"Things always go wrong in a war. Paco knows that, even if you don't."

"Renalto's not to blame. He warned me it would be dangerous."

"Dangerous? My God, you could have been beaten

to death or gang raped before he got there. Don't you know how little time it takes to— Turn around and look at me, dammit."

She didn't want to look at him. The fierceness in his voice hurt her too much and she didn't want to see that same unforgiving fierceness in his expression. But it had to be done sometime. She carefully put the brush down on the rocky ground beside her, stood up, and turned to face him.

He looked different. It wasn't only the clean uniform and the fact that his long hair had been cut several inches and no longer flowed down his back. That aura of indomitable strength that he had been forced to keep suppressed while he had been a prisoner was now almost visible to the naked eye. She felt as if she could reach out and touch it. Her gaze lifted to his face and she shivered. His expression was as forbidding as she had thought it would be. His dark eyes were glittering and his lips set in a thin line. Her glance quickly shifted to the top button of his shirt. "Why dwell on possibilities? Nothing irreparable occurred."

"It seems we have a difference of opinion. If I remember correctly, I took your virginity. I'd say that was irreparable."

"We've discussed that before. I don't see why you bring it up again." She shrugged. "It's not important. It would have happened some time or another."

"Not in a prison cell."

"It didn't matter. You were very . . . kind to me."

"Kind?" He looked at her in disbelief. "I tried to make it bearable for you, but there was no way I was kind. I drank you like a man dying of thirst in the desert."

She smiled faintly. "As I remember it, you made

sure I was equally thirsty before you indulged yourself." She straightened her shoulders and raised her
eyes to his. "And you're not really angry that we
were forced to . . . do that, is it? You don't like the
fact that I tricked you, that I made Jurado take us
out of the cell block to the interrogation room."

He nodded grimly. "You're damn right I am. You
gave me no choice."

"And by denying you that choice, we managed to
get you out of prison."

"At a considerable sacrifice to yourself." His black
eyes glittered down at her. "And I wasn't permitted
to decide whether I wanted to accept that sacrifice.
You forced it on me."

"Would you have accepted it?"

He was silent a moment. "No."

"That's what Renalto said you'd decide. The
defense rests."

"The hell it does." He covered the distance
between them and grasped her shoulders. "I decide
what price is worth my freedom."

"Or your life?"

"Or my life."

"Your gratitude certainly isn't overwhelming." She
tried to shrug off his grasp. "Would you mind letting
me go? You're hurting me. One of the whip strokes
must have struck my shoulder."

He released her so quickly, she staggered back.

"Lord, I'm sorry." His voice was hoarse. "I forgot
for a moment." He reached into his pocket and drew
out a small jar. "Turn around and take off your
shirt."

She didn't move.

He smiled crookedly. "It's a little late for modesty

now. I know every curve and facet of your body, down to that little mole in the hollow of your back."

She felt heat suffuse her body as she remembered when Ricardo had discovered that mole, his voice murmuring behind her while the water of the shower pounded down on them. "Circumstances are different now."

"Yes, they are. I won't deny it." He reached out and began to unbutton her shirt. She inhaled sharply as his hard knuckles brushed her upper breasts. His gaze flew to her face and for an instant he didn't move, his hand pressing against her flesh. Then he glanced away and quickly finished unbuttoning the shirt. "It's an entirely new situation." He turned her around to face the spring. "Let the shirt fall to your waist." She obeyed and she heard the sound of a jar being unscrewed behind her. "We have a whole new battery of choices to make."

"I don't agree. What happened in the cell has nothing to do with—"

"You won't need the bandages any longer, but I'll have to apply the ointment every day after your bath." He began to smooth the salve carefully into the raw flesh. "The caverns are damp and not the cleanest place in the world."

"I said I didn't agree," she persisted. "Why aren't you listening to me?"

"Because I know what you're going to say and I don't want to hear it." He knelt on the ground behind her and began to rub the ointment into the stripes on her lower back. He murmured, "The bastard brought the blood here, but the wound's already scabbed over."

"All I'm saying is that we're back to the point we were when I first walked into that cell," she said, trying to ignore the warmth generating through her body in fanlike waves wherever he touched her flesh. "And we have to look at what happened between us clearly."

"I'm looking at what happened with great clarity. It's amazing how clearly you see everything when a woman is being whipped to death before your eyes." His voice thickened. "Do you know how I felt as I stood there watching them beat you, not able to show a flicker of feeling because I knew that would only make Jurado hurt you more?"

"It must have been very difficult for you."

"I felt as if I were being torn to pieces." His voice lowered until it was barely audible. "I wanted to kill them and snatch you away and take you somewhere no one would ever hurt you again."

The rancho. Tall green grass and a lake with water lilies floating on its mirrored surface.

"So don't expect me to be grateful that you let yourself be put through that hell for my sake. I'd rather have rotted in that place than stood there and watched them do that to you." Suddenly his warm lips brushed the sensitive flesh at the hollow of her spine. "Never again, Lara," he whispered.

Her lungs contracted; her lips parted to take in more air. Her knees felt suddenly weak and she had to force herself to stand upright. "It was my choice." She hurriedly drew her shirt back over her shoulders and began to button it with trembling fingers. "And I didn't do it for you. I did it for Brett." She turned to face him and found him still on his knees. The position should have diminished him, but somehow it didn't. She doubted if anything could make him seem less than he was. "And that's who we have to talk about."

"Brett?" He shook his head. "I told you I couldn't make his choices for him."

"You can." Her hands closed into fists at her sides. "Don't spout your blasted philosophy to me now. If what I did at the Abbey has value at all to you, you'll give me your promise."

He flinched. "Lord, you're tough."

"I want to keep my brother safe. Give me your promise."

"I can't."

She looked at him in disbelief. "Don't you have enough wide-eyed children like Manuel in your army? Do you have to have Brett too?"

He paled. "Manuel doesn't fight. What do you think I am?"

"The Pied Piper. Why didn't you leave him in that village instead of bringing him here?"

"María sent word that the secret police suspected I'd placed him with her. Do I have to tell you what would have happened to María and Manuel if I hadn't brought them here?"

She wearily shook her head. "No, I guess I can see why you had to do it." She met his gaze. "But that has nothing to do with Brett." She tucked her shirt into her trousers. "Tell me what I can do to keep you from getting him killed in your damn war."

"It may be over before he's well enough to return."

"And it may not. It's gone on for nine years."

"I can't interfere with his free choice. I've fought a war to preserve that principle." He held up his hand as she opened her lips to speak. "But I can put him in a unit that will see a minimum of action." He paused. "And I can promise to protect him with my life if he does return."

It wasn't what she wanted, but it might be enough

to keep Brett safe. "And will you promise to do that?"

"Yes." He gazed at her directly. "If you'll also make me a promise."

She looked at him inquiringly.

"You must choose to stay with me."

She became still. "Stay with you?"

The corner of his mouth lifted in a crooked smile. "Do you think I don't know you wish only to run back to the States and forget Saint Pierre and I ever existed? I can't let you do that, Lara."

She gazed at him, stunned. "Why not?"

He met her gaze. "Because I love you."

Shock and an emotion she refused to identify soared through her. "You couldn't."

"I do."

She vigorously shook her head. "It was propinquity and a situation that—"

"I do." He rose to his feet. "I know myself and what I feel. At first, it was lust and an instinct to protect. But it became something else somewhere along the way."

"I don't love you," she whispered. "I won't love you."

He nodded. "I know. I'm at the opposite end of the pole from what you want for yourself. But it doesn't matter. I've learned to take what I can get." He shrugged. "Hell, I'll be lucky if I manage to live through the next few months. I want something of my own before I die."

Ricardo die? Pain jagged through her. "You're not being fair. That's emotional blackmail."

"I didn't mean it in that way. I only want to make you understand." He took a step toward her, speaking softly, urgently. "We'll be launching a major campaign before the month is over. Give me that month."

"You want me to stay here in the caverns?"

"It's the safest place for you." He cupped her cheek in his hand. "I'll take care of you. I promise nothing will happen to you, if you stay with me." He brushed back the hair from her temple with an infinitely gentle hand. "Please, *querida*, you won't regret it."

He was wrong; she would regret it. She felt the panic rising by the second as she looked up at him. She had been with him only two days and in that time he had managed to move her to pity, admiration, and lust. How the devil could you fight the Pied Piper with his magic flute? "I can't stay. It's sex. You only want me." She took a hasty step back. "It's not love."

For an instant she thought she saw a flicker of pain on his face before it hardened. "If you want to think so." He stood quietly, gazing at her. "But you will stay, Lara."

She looked at him incredulously. "You'd force me to stay?"

His lips twisted. "I told you that we have a new battery of choices to make. You made certain of that when you chose to come to the Abbey to rescue me." He paused. "We made love several times that night. How do you know that you're not with child?"

She didn't know and had been afraid to think about it. "It's not likely."

"Neither of us can know that and I don't choose to let you run away when you may be carrying my child."

"*Your* child? It would be my child."

"Our child." His smile was bittersweet. "And if the baby exists, it would open an entire new range of decisions to make. I fully intend to make them together. You'll stay here until we know one way or the other."

She laughed incredulously. "So that's why you want me to stay. I may be a brood mare for the great liberator."

"No!" He drew a deep breath and said with less violence, "I suppose you'll have to think what you like. I should have known you'd try to erect walls between us."

"I don't have to erect them; they already exist."

"Can't you see that I have to know? Everything that's ever belonged to me has been destroyed and I can't bear the thought that I might have destroyed you too."

"A baby wouldn't destroy me."

"But it would hurt you. Lord, I don't want to hurt you any more, Lara. I don't think I could stand it."

His tone was so anguished, for a moment she felt a twinge of sympathy pierce the anger she was feeling. She mustn't feel sorry for him, she thought desperately. If she let in one breath of softness, she might as well give up the fight. "You don't want to hurt me, but you're threatening me?"

His lips tightened. "Yes."

"With what exactly?"

He hesitated. "I could send a message to Brett that I need him."

Her eyes widened. "You bastard. He's still in a wheelchair."

He smiled bitterly. "But you seem to think I'm some kind of wizard. Surely all I'd need to do is snap my fingers and he'd come running."

"He can't run. Your damn revolution almost crippled him." Her fingernails bit into her palms. "But, yes, he'd come if you snapped your fingers."

"Then don't make me do it. Let him stay safely in Barbados."

"You're right; you may not live more than the next few months. I may murder you myself."

"I expected you to be angry."

"Then your expectations have been abundantly fulfilled. I hope you didn't also expect me to jump into your bed?"

He shook his head. "I want you, but it's your choice, Lara."

"I'm getting very tired of that word. I seem to have no choice at all in this particular matter."

"We always have choices," he said. "For instance, you could do as you threatened and murder me."

She stared at him in bewilderment. He appeared perfectly serious. "And have your followers tear me apart."

"Paco would try to protect you."

"If he didn't kill me himself. He loves you."

"True." He shrugged. "But he likes you and there's a possibility you could end the revolution and your dilemma with one blow."

"I think you must be crazy."

"I'm only showing you that there are always choices."

"Not one I'm willing to take. I'm no murderer. I couldn't . . ." She trailed off and shook her head. "I'll find another way to win."

"I forgot for a moment how much you hate to lose." A ghost of a smile touched his lips. "I don't want you to lose either. I just want to protect you and my child." He turned away. "I'll send Manuel in to you. He'll show you around the caverns and introduce you to my officers. We'll try to make your stay as comfortable and pleasant as possible. I'll be busy a good deal of the time for the next few days, but I'll try to get away for dinner."

"I don't want to see you."

He glanced back over his shoulder. "But I want to see you," he said softly. "I just want to be with you. Don't worry; you don't even have to speak to me."

He was gone before she could reply. She stood looking after him, her emotions in a tumult. It was anger, she told herself desperately. She was angry and frustrated, and this aching inside had nothing to do with pity or the strange bonding forged between them in those days together. She wouldn't allow herself to feel anything else for him.

What she was feeling had to be anger.

The caverns were huge and comprised of a multitude of natural chambers like the one in which Lara had regained consciousness. In spite of its spaciousness, Ricardo's forces seemed to occupy every foot of it. While Manuel was showing her through the cave, they encountered any number of officers, but they all reacted with impeccable courtesy when Manuel introduced her to them. The entire area had an air of bustle, a vibrant aliveness that was in sharp contrast to the hollow dimness of the caverns.

"How do you manage not to get lost?" Lara asked Manuel after following him through seemingly endless winding corridors. "I think you'd better give me some bread crumbs to drop whenever you can't come with me."

Manuel glanced at her with a puzzled frown. "Bread crumbs?"

"You know, the Hansel and Gretel fairy tale."

His expression was still uncomprehending.

Lara felt a pang of sympathy as she realized he was unfamiliar with the story. Poor baby, there had probably been little opportunity in his life for fairy tales. "Never mind, I'll tell you later. Are we finished with the grand tour?"

"Almost." Manuel's pace quickened as he headed for an opening at the end of the corridor. "You must meet Dr. Salazar. The chamber up ahead is the doctor's infirmary."

"An infirmary?"

"That's what he calls it. It has many pallets and even a table for operations."

She shivered. "It sounds like something from the Dark Ages."

"It's all we have." Manuel looked at her over his shoulder. "And the doctor is much respected. He was present at Ricardo's birth."

"A kind of court physician for the great liberator?" Lara asked dryly.

Manuel's expression became troubled as he paused in the arched opening of the infirmary. "I don't understand you. You saved Ricardo and yet you speak as if you don't like him."

"Don't worry about it," Lara said gently. "What I feel for your Ricardo is a little complicated. He made me very angry."

"How can that be? Everyone loves Ricardo Lázaro."

"So I've been told, but sometimes I don't agree with the consensus of—"

"Ah, Señorita Clavel, you look much better than when I last saw you." The tall, spare man approaching them was dressed in the same green fatigues as the other soldiers she had seen, but his graying hair and the crow's-feet fanning his bright eyes proclaimed him to be nearing sixty. "I'm Dr. Juan Salazar. I tended your back when Ricardo brought you here two days ago."

"You must have done an excellent job." Lara found herself returning the man's warm smile. "The wounds are only a little sore now."

"I always do an excellent job." Salazar's dark eyes twinkled. "It's Mother Nature and my patients who fail me, not I them."

Lara chuckled as she looked around the large chamber. Thirty or forty pallets lay at regular intervals on the stone floor, but only four of them were occupied. The area appeared bright and pristine in spite of its primitive accoutrements. "Manuel said this was your infirmary."

He shrugged. "I do the best I can. It's not much. I can only patch them up and send them to Barbados for more extensive treatment."

"You don't seem very busy right now."

"Thank God." He smiled sardonically. "We're between campaigns, but we'll have more than enough to keep our hands full when Ricardo launches a raid."

She kept her gaze carefully averted. "Is that going to be soon?"

"Probably. Ricardo never waits long to start events moving."

She felt a frisson of fear, which she quickly suppressed. She forced a smile. "Well, then it's a good thing this particular patient is fully recovered."

The doctor nodded. "But you shouldn't try to do too much right away. The psychological shock of such an experience can fell you even as the physical wounds heal."

"I'll be fine. Is there anything I can do to help you? I can't just sit around and twiddle my thumbs."

Salazar permitted himself a small smile. "Ricardo said you'd react like that when you started to heal."

"Oh, did he?" She frowned. "He obviously thinks he knows me very well."

"Which annoys you." Salazar studied her defiant expression thoughtfully. "It shouldn't, you know. Ricardo's the best judge of character I've ever seen. In his position he's had to be, and he's perfected the art until he's close to being a mind reader."

"I've noticed."

"She doesn't like him," Manuel said flatly.

Salazar laughed. "Then she'll be very good for the rascal. He needs a challenge." His gaze met Lara's. "Ricardo said you'd be staying for a while."

"It appears I have little choice."

Salazar ignored the curtness of her reply. "And I can always use help."

She frowned with sudden uncertainty. "You'll have to teach me. I'm afraid I don't have any nursing experience."

"You'll get plenty of it around here," he said grimly. "I have two regular nurses, but they're usually worked off their feet. If you can do what you're told, you'll help fill the gap."

"I can try," Lara said. "When do I start?"

"Not until you're fully well. Ricardo would give me fits if I used you now."

"You didn't appear intimidated by him before."

"Not by Ricardo, the man; but Ricardo, the general, is another kettle of fish entirely."

"I'll be back tomorrow morning," she said firmly.

"I told you, Ricardo would—" He broke off and chuckled as he saw her determined expression. "Very well. Why not? But you'll have to be the one to do battle with him. I'm too old."

"With great pleasure," she said with precision. "A battle sounds very inviting at the moment. Goodbye, Dr. Salazar." She turned to leave. "Come on, Manuel; I need you to lead me back to home base."

Manuel nodded. "And I must prepare your chamber."

"Prepare?"

"Ricardo said you must be made very comfortable."

She glanced back at the spartan furnishings of the infirmary. "Comfort doesn't seem a very plentiful commodity in these caverns."

"I can do it." Manuel started down the twisting path at a trot. "Trust me."

Five

Manuel set to work with enthusiasm and ingenuity. Before the day was over, Lara found her small, bare cubicle transformed. In the first two hours he managed to conjure two air mattresses, clean blankets, and even the luxury of clean cotton sheets. A short time later three additional lanterns, two water canteens, and eight well-thumbed paperback novels appeared. During the next four hours luxuries and necessities dribbled into the chamber at a steady flow, sometimes brought by Manuel, sometimes by one of the soldiers, who smiled shyly, set their treasures down, and vanished as quickly as they had appeared.

Lara finally called a halt to it. "Enough," she said firmly as Manuel set down a handgun and a walkie-talkie on the pile of blankets in the corner. "Where are you getting all this, Manuel?"

"Some from supplies, some from the soldiers." Manuel grinned cheerfully. "Don't worry; I didn't steal any of it. Everyone wants to make sure you have all you need. All I had to do was ask."

"What on earth am I going to do with a gun and a walkie-talkie?"

"Everyone has a gun." Manuel's brow furrowed in thought before he suddenly smiled triumphantly. "And with the walkie-talkie you could talk to Ricardo when he's in the war room."

Lara shook her head. "I don't need all of this."

Manuel's face fell with disappointment. "I didn't do well?"

"You did too well," Lara said gently. "And I thank you very much, but it has to stop."

"But I didn't get you a pack of playing cards yet."

"I'm sure the soldiers need their cards more than I do."

Manuel stubbornly shook his head. "Ricardo said you must have—"

"No more." Lara hurriedly changed the subject as she saw him start to protest. "But I'm very hungry. When do we have dinner?"

Manuel was immediately distracted. "The soldiers eat in the mess, but you'll be served here with Ricardo."

"I can eat with the soldiers. I'm sure you don't have the—"

"The lady is hungry, Manuel." Ricardo stood in the arched opening. "Run along and fetch us something to eat."

Manuel nodded eagerly. "Right away." He darted toward the doorway. "You must talk to her, Ricardo. She won't take the playing cards."

Ricardo's gaze never left Lara's face. "I'll talk to her."

Manuel disappeared from view.

Lara pulled her glance away from Ricardo. "He's very determined."

"But evidently a better scavenger than I thought. You have the caverns' equivalent to the lap of luxury here."

"He must be very persuasive." She moved across the chamber and dropped down on the folded blankets with which Manuel had formed a seat. "And I'm surprised he speaks such good English."

"The good doctor. He conducts classes in English when his work permits. After the revolution we'll have close ties with the United States, and the more citizens who speak English, the better for them."

"I like your Dr. Salazar."

"You like him; you like Paco; you like Manuel." He enumerated lightly. "I seem to be the only one in your bad graces."

"And you're going to remain there." She met his gaze directly. "I don't like blackmail."

"Neither do I." He sat down across from her. "It's necessary, Lara."

"In your opinion."

"In my opinion," he agreed. "That's all I've been able to rely on for years. I can't afford to change my modus operandi now."

He was sitting quietly, his hands linked over his knees, the way she had seen him sit for hours in the cell—the same stillness, the same air of repressed force and authority, the same graceful sensuality. He was doing absolutely nothing to engender a sexual response in her and yet the response was suddenly there, alive and tingling between them. Her heart pounded crazily; the cotton of her shirt was abrasive against her hardening nipples as her breasts lifted and fell with her quickened breathing. She looked away from him again, trying to keep her expression unrevealing. "I told you I didn't want you here."

"I have to have my chance."

"To get me in the sack again?" she asked flippantly.

He didn't answer for so long that she lifted her gaze back to his face. His expression was controlled and yet she knew instinctively that she had hurt him. It shouldn't matter to her, she thought.

Yet it did matter. His pain made her ache in some mysterious way she didn't understand.

"Yes, I want to make love to you again." His voice was thick. "I want it so much that I'm hurting right now. I keep thinking of how tight and hot you felt when I was moving in and out of you. And the sounds you made when I put my—"

"I don't want to hear it." The color blazed in her cheeks. "It's over."

He shook his head. "It's not over. If it were over, I wouldn't be sitting here wanting you, and you wouldn't be sitting there wanting me."

She wouldn't lie. "You were my first lover. Naturally, I'm still curious about—" She broke off. "But it's not going to happen."

"I think it will. I hope it will." He smiled crookedly. "But even if it doesn't, I'll not lose this time, Lara. Do you know why?"

She didn't answer.

"Because it's not only the sex. Don't you know that I enjoyed sitting in that cell watching your face when we were playing games almost as much as I did when I made love to you?"

She gazed at him in disbelief.

He chuckled. "It's true. You notice I said 'almost.'

The pleasure wasn't as intense or explosive, but it . . . warmed me."

She understood what he meant. She had to fight that warmth, more dangerous than lust, that flooded through her at his words.

"So I'll win just by being with you." His smile faded. "I think that if you'll let yourself, you'll win too. We leapt over a hell of a lot of hurdles in that cell."

"I won't let myself," she said. "I can't let myself feel anything for you, Ricardo."

He stiffened. "Because of your dreams of that little house and big dogs and everything neat and tidy? Well, my life isn't neat and tidy, and I doubt if it will ever be."

"That's what I'm trying to tell you. We're *different*."

He silently shook his head.

"We are," she insisted.

"Only because you choose to be. You can always choose a new path."

"What about you? You could choose a new path."

He smiled. "Touché. You're right. I'm not being fair. I could choose to give up the revolution and follow you to your small town. Do you think I should?"

She stared at him, disconcerted by the question. "No."

"Why not?"

She had answered instinctively and now she had to think about it. "Because you *are* the revolution. Because your beliefs make you what you are, make you do what you do."

"Your beliefs made you come to the Abbey to rescue me."

"But only to save Brett and take him away from you."

"Are you sure?" He looked thoughtfully down at his linked fingers. "Wouldn't there have been other, less dangerous ways to accomplish the same end?"

"I didn't see any other way."

"Think about it." He raised his gaze to her face. "I don't think you're the woman you believe you are."

"You said that before." She shook her head. "And you're wrong."

"Perhaps," he said. "But think about it anyway."

He had given her too much to think about already. Her body was responding as mindlessly to him as it had when she had first met him, and she couldn't afford to yield him any more victories. "If you come here again, I won't speak to you." Desperation threaded her voice. "You might as well give up now."

"I'll still come." He met her gaze and she saw both implacable will and an odd hint of sadness in his expression. "And I won't give up, Lara."

He stayed for the simple dinner Manuel brought them and then departed.

He came again the next evening and the following night also.

Lara tried to maintain a frigid silence, but he ignored her coldness. He didn't speak of the war or his life of the last nine years, but of that time before the revolution. He painted vivid pictures of his days on the rancho where he had grown up and then spoke of his time at the university. The tales intrigued her in spite of herself and she found herself drawn to question him.

"You never speak of your parents," she said. "Did you have a close relationship?"

"Not with my mother." He shrugged. "She liked being the lady of the rancho, but motherhood was a bit of a strain. I can't really blame her. I was as wild a hellion as you could imagine when I was growing up. But my father and I were close. He was a good, simple man with strong convictions. He saw no reason to hide them when the junta came into power. He should have known—" He broke off and lifted his cup of coffee to his lips. "I admired him."

"He died in the revolution?"

"Before the revolution. When I was at the university. The junta ordered my mother and him taken to the Abbey and the rancho confiscated." He looked down into the coffee in his cup. "They were shot before my eyes."

Shock jolted through Lara. "Dear God," she whispered.

"I'd been agitating against the junta at the university and they wanted to show me what could happen if I continued. So they took me to the Abbey and—"

"Don't talk about it," she said quickly. "You don't have to tell me."

He shook his head. "I want you to know. It's part of what I am." His grip tightened on the cup in his hand. "The junta handled the matter very stupidly. I was only nineteen and all they would have had to tell me was that they wouldn't kill them if I'd stop agitating. I loved my father."

Lara swallowed to ease the tightness in her throat. "They didn't give you that choice?"

He shook his head. "They wanted to set an example. They wouldn't listen to me. They shot them and let me go back to the university with orders to disband our group or the same thing would happen to me and all my friends." He smiled sadly. "As I said, they handled the matter very stupidly. They should have killed me too."

"No!" Lara's rejection came with instinctive force. How many times during his lifetime had Ricardo been on the verge of death? While she had been plodding steadily forward in her comfortable, mundane world, he had been going through hellish mental and physical anguish.

"I was like a madman. Full of rage . . . and guilt."

"Guilt?"

"They told me that I had killed them. That my rabble-rousing speeches had sent them to their deaths. For a while I believed them." He put his cup down on the rocky ground. "But then I realized that they would have been killed anyway. My father was a powerful man and he hated the junta as much as I did."

"So you started the revolution."

"No one starts a revolution; it's a chain reaction that explodes and keeps on exploding until the end is reached."

"With you providing the nitroglycerine."

"Do you think I like it?" he asked with sudden fierceness. "Do you think I wouldn't rather have spent my youth doing something besides fighting this damn war? I'm almost thirty and I've known nothing but killing and maiming." He drew a deep breath. "Some things are worth fighting for, but, Lord, I'm tired of it all."

"But you still go on with it."

"As you'd go on if something threatened your brother."

"He's my family, all I've got."

"And Saint Pierre is my family, and the people fighting for it are all I've got." He met her gaze. "You love your brother very much?"

She nodded. "We're twins and sometimes I feel as if we're one person. Oh, we have character differences, but we usually are alike on most major issues."

He smiled. "Except me."

"Except you."

A silence fell between them before Ricardo changed the subject. "Juan Salazar told me today you've been working in the infirmary."

"Not to help your revolution," she said quickly. "I just can't stand doing nothing."

"I'm not foolish enough to think I have a convert," he said softly. "I only want you to take it easy. Have you been sleeping well?"

"Yes." She made a face. "As well as possible with all these stalactites hovering over me. I feel as if I'm a victim in the *Pit and the Pendulum*."

"I've felt like that myself at times." He rose to his feet. "But you haven't had dreams about what happened to you in prison? No sudden depressions or periods when you get the shakes?"

She shook her head. "Dr. Salazar asked me that too. I think I'm a little insulted that you both think I'm such a wimp."

He suddenly grinned. "I wouldn't presume. We just know that sometimes you don't get rid of the psychological baggage with the situation."

"You seem to have survived considerably worse than I went through with no aftereffects."

"I put on a good front." His grin vanished. "If you start having problems, tell me."

"I'll handle it."

He swore under his breath. "Why the hell should you? What happened to you is my responsibility."

"The devil it is. I came down here to your little tropical paradise of my own free will. If you want to play Atlas and carry the entire island of Saint Pierre on your shoulders, go ahead. But leave me out of it. I'll take care of myself, thank you."

His frown vanished and a reluctant smile curved his lips. "Okay. I won't carry you on my shoulders. That isn't the portion of my anatomy I want close to you anyway." His smile became blatantly sensual as his voice lowered to a seductive murmur. "Do you know how I'd like to carry you? I'd like to be deep inside you, with those lovely legs wound around my hips."

Heat tingled through her as she looked up at him. During the past hour she had been filled with a multitude of strong emotions toward him varying from poignant sympathy to indignation. She had thought she had her physical responses to him firmly under control, but now she realized it had been Ricardo who had damped down that powerful chemical attraction between them.

"Yes." He met her gaze. "It's still there and it won't go away. I think about it every night before I go to sleep. Do you?"

She moistened her lips with her tongue. "No, I don't let myself."

"It hurts me, too, but I let you in anyway," he said softly. "I could no more close you out than I could my own thoughts."

"Ricardo, it's no *use*."

"Do you remember what you said about your brother and the way you sometimes thought of the two of you as one person? Well, we're like that, Lara.

Sometimes I feel so close to you that I can read your thoughts."

She laughed shakily. "I've noticed. But then everyone knows you're some kind of mind reader and magician. It has nothing to do with us. I certainly can't tell what you're thinking."

"You could if you wanted to," he continued urgently. "Look at me, Lara. What am I thinking now?"

Pain. Desire. Tenderness. Love.

No, not love. He couldn't love her, just as she couldn't love him. She hurriedly looked away from him. "I don't know and I don't want to know. I won't let you hypnotize me into believing what you want me to believe. You're too darn good at this razzle-dazzle."

"It's not razzle-dazzle." He paused before adding simply, "It's love, Lara."

"No! I won't have it. I won't love you."

"Perhaps not." He reached down and ran his index finger along the line of cheekbone. "But you can't stop me from loving you, *querida*."

"Can't you see how unreasonable you're being? We're nothing alike. We don't even want the same way of life."

"But we want each other; we love each other."

"No."

His hand fell away from her face and he turned away. "Good night, Lara."

"Why won't you listen to me?"

He didn't answer as he strode from the chamber.

Lara could still feel the warmth of his finger on the flesh of her cheek, and loneliness swept through her. It was the same loneliness she had felt last night and the night before when he had left her.

Dear heaven, she was becoming so conditioned to his presence, she realized with a sharp jab of fear. She was dissatisfied when he wasn't with her. All through the day when she had been working with Dr. Salazar, she'd been aware of a new sense of excitement filling her at the thought of Ricardo coming to her for these hours in the evening. She had scarcely allowed herself to acknowledge her feelings, but now she could no longer deny them. She had looked on these hours with Ricardo as the highlight of the day and she had felt a deep contentment just being with the dratted man.

Let it be lust, she prayed.

But Ricardo had not made any attempt to arouse her until that last moment before he had left. She felt sympathy for him because of the loneliness and sorrow he had known, she rationalized. Of course she respected the strong man who had emerged from the struggle. And of course she admired his intelligence, his wit, his devotion to his country. But none of those qualities filled her with such glowing warmth when she was with him.

He was becoming much too important to her.

When he came to her tomorrow evening she must be constantly on her guard against him.

Ricardo didn't come to her the next evening.

Manuel served her meal with somber efficiency and largely in silence. He didn't mention either Ricardo or his absence.

Lara had no intention of mentioning Ricardo either. She should be happy he hadn't come tonight, she told herself. She had been bracing herself for their encounter all evening and now she evidently had no cause to worry. Yet she did worry.

She was halfway through the meal when she finally broke down and asked Manuel, "Where is he?"

The child avoided her gaze. "Have some of the melon. It's very good tonight."

"Where's Ricardo, Manuel?"

He stood up. "I'll get your coffee."

"I don't want any coffee. I want to know where Ricardo is this evening."

Manuel hesitated, his expression troubled. "He told me not to tell you."

"Why not?"

He shrugged and left the chamber.

Another woman.

She stiffened as the sudden thought sent a shock wave through her. Jurado had said Ricardo was a very earthy man. Now that he was back with his people it was perfectly natural that he should indulge his sexual appetites. She had seen several voluptuous women with the soldiers in the caverns and knew he needed only to crook his finger and they would come running. There was no reason why she should feel this sense of pain and betrayal. Ricardo Lázaro didn't belong to her and she had no right to feel this raging primitive jealousy.

And it *was* jealousy. And it was primitive . . . raging. The thought of Ricardo locked between the thighs of one of those dusky women made her head swim with anger. She wanted to murder the bit—

"Señorita, come quick!" Manuel was standing in the doorway. "Dr. Salazar needs you."

Lara jumped to her feet. "What's wrong?"

"The wounded are coming in."

Lara moved hurriedly toward him. "Wounded?"

"From the raid." Manuel darted down the corridor in the direction of the infirmary, shouting over his shoulder, "Many deaths, many wounded. Hurry."

"What raid? Manuel, tell—"

He was gone and Lara started down the corridor after him at a dead run, her heart pounding so hard, she thought it would leap from her breast.

Wounded. Dead. Ricardo!

The huge infirmary chamber echoed with the groans of men in pain and Salazar's sharp, decisive orders as she ran into the room. At least thirty of the pallets were filled with casualties and Salazar's two nurses were working with frantic haste, moving from patient to patient, adjusting an IV bottle here, applying a pressure bandage there.

"Lara. Good." Salazar gave her a glance over his shoulder as he inserted a hypodermic needle into the arm of the man on the pallet before him. "Go wash up and then give Luz and María a hand. Heaven knows, they'll need a dozen more before this night's over."

"What happened?" Lara asked.

"A raid on the Abbey. You'll be glad to know the good Captain Jurado is no longer with us." He began cutting away the soldier's blood-soaked shirt. "According to Paco, they left the Abbey a mass of burning rubble."

"Paco? What about Ricardo?"

"Ricardo led the attack."

"Is he okay?"

"Probably."

"What do you mean 'probably'?" Panic raced through Lara, robbing her of breath and reason. "Is he safe?"

"I haven't seen him. Paco lost sight of him after the first assault. He's gone back to look for him."

"How could they lose sight of him?" Lara grasped Salazar's arm. "He's their leader, dammit. How could—"

"Don't you think I, too, want to know Ricardo is safe? But there are men dying and I can't stop and go searching for him. I have to rely on Paco." He added impatiently, not looking at her, "Now, go help Luz and María."

Lara turned and moved dazedly toward the two nurses. Ricardo had led the attack. In her mind's eye she could see that deadly machine gun on the roof of the Abbey spitting down death and bullets. Over thirty men were lying here wounded, perhaps dying here in this chamber. If Ricardo had led the attack, wouldn't he have been one of the first to go down?

"I'll be lucky if I manage to live through the next few months."

Her terror grew as she remembered Ricardo's words.

"I want something of my own . . ."

She wanted to weep; she wanted to run through the caverns looking for Ricardo. She couldn't do either. Like the doctor, she had to rely on Paco. In the meantime, men were wounded and dying and she was needed.

She paused beside María and asked quietly, "What can I do to help?"

Lara worked steadily for over eight hours without knowing whether Ricardo was dead or alive. Just as she was leaving the infirmary in the early-morning hours, she looked up from sponging down a young soldier to see Ricardo standing in the doorway talking to Salazar.

Waves of joy crashed over her, and she was suddenly dizzy and disoriented.

He was alive!

Ricardo's dark hair was tousled and his face soot-stained and he appeared weary to the point of exhaustion, but, by all that was holy, he was alive!

He must have felt her staring at him. He looked away from the doctor and met her gaze. He stopped speaking and just stared at her.

She should turn her head. He was seeing too much. She felt transparent, more vulnerable than she'd ever been before.

Then he smiled at her, a brilliant, loving smile that took her breath away. She found her lips curving in a joyous answering smile.

She couldn't take her eyes off him. She didn't even tell herself how foolish she was being to let him see her happiness. Subterfuge was unable to survive the deluge of relief pouring through her.

He was alive.

Ricardo stood for a moment, smiling at her. Then he murmured something to Salazar, turned, and strode out of the infirmary.

Six

Lara slept for a solid ten hours after her nursing shift.

Ricardo was sitting cross-legged on the ground beside her pallet when she opened her eyes.

Happiness shimmered through her as she smiled drowsily up at him. "You look considerably cleaner than you did the last time I saw you," she whispered. "Your face was all sooty."

"I took a bath." He lifted a mocking brow. "A regular occurrence actually."

"That's what I need." She yawned and sat up. "I was too tired to do anything but fall into bed when I left the infirmary."

"I could see you were exhausted when I dropped in last night." He reached out and brushed back a strand of hair from her forehead. "And I think I saw something else as well."

"Did you?" She instinctively scooted back away from him. "I don't know what you—"

"Don't put up the barriers again." He smiled at

her, a smile so loving, she felt her wariness melt away. "It's too late."

"I . . . was glad you were alive."

"So was I. In that moment I was more glad to be alive than I've ever been before."

She shook her head. "Don't do this. You're pushing me. It's all too quick. I don't know what I'm feeling. I have to think."

"I have to push you. I'm trying to consolidate my position before you change your mind."

She looked away from him. "Why did you attack the Abbey? You said there weren't many prisoners left there."

"Enough. The next major offensive may push us over the top and the first thing Jurado would do is murder the prisoners. I wanted Jurado and that hellhole destroyed." He ran his hand down her neck and a hot shiver followed his touch. "And I wanted to erase him from your life and memory as if he had never been born."

"Killing someone can't do that."

"I know. But you'll never have to worry about him touching you again. I couldn't erase the memory of him from your past, but you'll never have to face him in your future." He didn't give her a chance to answer as he took her hand and pulled her to her feet. "Take your bath and then get something to eat. I'll see you tomorrow."

"Tomorrow?" She couldn't keep the disappointment from her voice. "Where are you going?"

"Nowhere. You said I was moving too fast. I'm just giving you space. I can afford to let you have a little respite from my presence now." He met her gaze. "Of course, if you decide you don't want the space, you know where I am."

She didn't know where he was, she realized. She had never been to his quarters. "I don't really know anything about you or what you do here when you're not with me." She frowned. "And you didn't even tell me you were going to raid the Abbey."

"I wasn't sure you'd be interested." He turned her around and gave her bottom an affectionate pat that propelled her toward the door. "I'm happy as hell to find out you are."

She realized then, to her disgust, that she was afraid to look at him. It was crazy to feel so painfully shy with a man with whom she had experienced the ultimate intimacy. "I'm interested." She cast him an anxious glance over her shoulder as a thought occurred to her. "You're telling me the truth? You're just giving me time? You're not going on another raid tonight?"

His expression softened. "I'm not going anywhere. I promise I'll be back here tomorrow."

Relief poured through her. "That's good." She smiled with an effort. "I'd just as soon you forget about battles and raids for the time being. I'm not much good at this nursing business and I don't like the prospect of spending another hellish night at the infirmary."

His voice was very gentle. "Juan says you did very well."

"He was desperate. The good doctor would have drafted an orangutan to help out if the ape was capable of holding a pressure bandage."

He laughed. "Perhaps. But you still filled his needs." He paused and his laughter faded. "As you filled mine. In spite of your protests, you persist in giving to us. I only wish we could stop taking and give in return. I *need* to give to you, Lara."

His stare was warmly intent and Lara felt that warmth enfolding her in a velvet cocoon. Her gaze clung to his face in helpless fascination. "I . . . have to take my bath."

She whirled and walked quickly away from him, her pace quickening to almost a run even before she went through the entranceway.

The spring-fed pool was frigid, as usual, but Lara's mind was in such a turmoil, she scarcely registered the temperature of the water.

She couldn't love him.

But she had felt a devastating sense of loss when she had thought he might be dead and when she *had* seen him. . . .

She closed her eyes, savoring the remembered moment of joy.

So she felt something for him. It didn't have to be love. They had grown very close through their experience at the Abbey. It was sex and companionship, not love. Naturally, she felt sympathy for a man who was living on the edge of danger. Naturally, she wanted to help him in any way she could.

Dear heaven, even to herself she sounded hypocritical and self-righteous, she thought self-deprecatingly. Why not admit he was a sexy, gorgeous man and she had a king-size yen? Since Ricardo obviously felt the same desire, wasn't it sensible to appease both their needs? There would be no harm in giving him what he wanted from her in these last days together.

She strode out of the water, grabbed a towel from the stony bank, and began to dry herself. She would go find Manuel and have him take her to Ricardo's quarters before she lost her nerve, she decided. She would explain everything very clearly to Ricardo so that there would be no misunderstanding and see what he had to say. She was being logical and there was no reason he shouldn't agree. Reaching for her shirt, she paused as a fleeting memory of that radiant joy she had felt when she had seen him in the infirmary came back to her. Relief. The emotion underlying joy had been relief and nothing else.

Lord, she hoped she wasn't lying to herself.

The massive uniformed guard who stood before Ricardo's quarters straightened as Lara and Manuel approached. Lara stopped in the corridor, hesitating.

"Don't worry," Manuel whispered as he pushed her forward. "He won't give you any trouble. All the soldiers know who you are."

"Do they?" If they did, then they had a distinct advantage, Lara thought nervously. At the moment she wasn't sure she knew who she was or what she was doing here. The "reasonable" decision she had made not thirty minutes before seemed brash and slightly mad now.

Manuel nodded gravely. "We all know you belong to Ricardo. The guard will let you pass."

"I don't belong—" She broke off and moved toward the entrance. "Are you coming?"

He didn't answer and when she glanced back over her shoulder, she found the child had vanished down the corridor from which they had come.

The big guard smiled benignly and let her pass through the arched doorway without a challenge.

Ricardo's quarters were starkly ascetic as she

could tell from only the most fleeting glance as she entered.

Ricardo was half sitting, half lying, on the pallet across the room, leaning back against the stone wall behind him, a gray woolen blanket draped carelessly across his hips.

He was naked.

She stopped, staring breathlessly at him. His body looked hard, lean, and tough, but there was nothing hard about his expression. Her heart was drumming so loud, she was sure he could hear it across the distance separating them. She swallowed to ease the dryness of her throat. "Hello."

He smiled, a warm, brilliant smile, and held out his hand. "Hello, *querida*."

It was going to be fine. He was no stranger. This was the Ricardo she had known in the cell, the Ricardo who had soothed and comforted her and built a beautiful world to shut out all the pain and sordidness. She moved toward him. "You seem to have been expecting me."

"Not expecting . . . only hoping you'd come." His dark eyes twinkled up at her as she knelt before him. "I wouldn't dare take you for granted. That last morning in the cell proved you're too dangerous a woman to assume anything about." He reached out and gently touched her lower lip with two fingers. "But I thought I'd be ready, just in case."

Her lip throbbed beneath the pads of his fingers. She drew a shaky breath. "This is crazy. I don't even know why I'm here."

"I do." He began to unbutton her green army shirt. "Let me show you."

She cast a glance at the open doorway. "What if—"

"No one will come in. I told Pedro to allow no one

but you past the door tonight." He parted the edges of her shirt and lay his hands there for a long moment, looking at her breasts. "Perfect." His hands grasped her shoulders and he slowly drew her toward him. "You're tense. Relax. This is right, Lara. You'll see how right it is." His fingers dug into her knotted shoulder muscles as his warm tongue caressed one pointed nipple. "Lord, how I've wanted this."

She gasped as his lips closed hungrily on the pink tip and he began a gentle suction. The sensation was indescribably erotic, his hands soothing and massaging away the tension while his mouth took and teased. The muscles of her stomach clenched and she instinctively arched toward him, offering more.

She cried out as he bit down with just enough force to send arousal tingling through every muscle and pore of her body.

"God, how I love to hear you when you—" His fingers were feverishly working at her belt, loosening her trousers. "Hurry, it's been too long."

She had meant to talk to him first, she remembered hazily. "I wanted to tell you . . . Ricardo, it's not—" She broke off as his hand slid into her trousers, down her stomach to cup her womanhood. His long, hard fingers were smoothing, exploring, rubbing, while his mouth enveloped her right breast. Later. She would talk to him later. Right now she had to have him within her.

"Take off your clothes, love." He lifted his head, his eyes glazed, feverish. "I need to see you. I need to—"

She was already shedding garments with lightning speed, as frantic as he was to join with him.

"I'm trying." She laughed shakily as she felt him begin a rhythmic stroking. "You're not—" Her spine arched upward as his fingers plunged deep. She closed her eyes and the last word came throatily. "Waiting."

"I *can't* wait. You're too tight. . . ." His chest was lifting and falling with the force of his breathing as he tossed the blanket aside and pulled her astraddle him. "To hell with the rest."

He sheathed her on his manhood with one deep thrust.

Her head fell back, her hair streaming down her back, as she felt him big, hard, alive within her. She wanted to scream, to pant, to move.

But his hands on her hips held her still, sealing himself deeply within her. She was conscious of the coarser male hair brushing the softness of her inner thighs, the swelling of her breasts, the low, keening cry welling from her throat as wave after wave of heat flowed over her. She felt possessed, helpless, bound to him.

Her eyes opened and she gazed dazedly down at his face. "Ricardo."

An expression of exquisite pleasure contorted his features. "It's so good it hurts, doesn't it?" he whispered. "We were meant to be together like this. Can't you feel it?"

Then he started to move, thrusting upward, shifting her for his pleasure and her own. The pace was furious, the depth intense, the emotional response pure madness.

Lara could feel the tears running down her cheeks as the tension mounted to fever pitch and beyond.

Ricardo cupped her breasts in his hands as his hips bucked forcefully upward, stallion wild, furnace hot—his expression absorbed, intent, as he gave her more than she dreamed she could take.

"Now, Lara." He closed his eyes, the thrusts growing harder, wilder with every breath. "Now!"

She cried out, every muscle convulsing as the fiery climax broke over her.

The release was so intense, she was only vaguely aware of Ricardo's low groan as he clutched her to him with breath-stealing force. She lay against him, dazed, dizzy, every muscle limp.

"Mine . . ." Ricardo's voice in her ear was so soft, it was almost inaudible. He gently stroked her hair back from her face as he murmured, "You belong to me now, *querida*."

Panic soared through her. She had to say something. She couldn't let him think— She tried to steady her breathing as she sat up again. "No, it's not like that." Her voice was trembling as she forced herself to look down at him. "I don't love you, Ricardo."

He became still. "You do love me."

She shook her head. "I care about you. Perhaps I'm a little infatuated with you, but I don't love you."

The joy vanished from his expression and it became shuttered again. He lifted her off his lap and set her on the pallet beside him. When he spoke, his tone was as guarded as the expression on his face. "Then may I ask why you decided to favor me with the gift of your body? You're not a woman who commits herself in this fashion merely for sex."

She found she was suddenly shivering and drew the wool blanket up to her shoulders. "You were alone. You said you wanted something of your own."

"Not a one-night stand." He smiled mirthlessly. "That's not what I was talking about."

"I wanted to make you happy." She nervously ran her fingers through her hair. "Oh, I don't know. I just didn't want you to be alone right now when you—" She stopped in mid sentence.

"When I might be killed?" He sat up and leaned against the stone wall, gazing at her without expression. "So you felt sorry for me and thought you'd throw me a bone."

"No, it wasn't like that."

"How was it? Tell me."

"I felt . . . " She stopped, moistening her lips with her tongue. "Why are you cross-examining me like this? Why can't you accept what we've had without analyzing it to death."

"Because I want a hell of a lot more than you're offering me." His tone was taut with leashed violence. "I don't want your damn pity. I want you to love me."

She gazed at him helplessly, her eyes glistening with tears.

His face softened and he smiled lopsidedly. "I said I needed to give to you, but evidently you're not ready to take what I have to give." He grimaced. "Well, I'd be a fool not to take what you're offering me at the moment. I gather you're willing to occupy my bed from now until the time I send you back to Barbados?"

She nodded silently.

"Then I accept the gift." His lips twisted. "Who am I to reject charity when it comes in such an appetizing package."

She had hurt him, she realized with aching regret. She had never meant to hurt Ricardo. His life had been tragic enough without her adding to his pain. She suddenly wanted to go back into his arms and hold him and tell him—

Tell him what? She had already yielded too much of herself and was surrendering more every moment she spent with him.

"Don't look so frightened." Ricardo's gaze narrowed on her face. "You've made me a promise. You can't back out now."

She smiled with an effort. "I'm not backing out. Why should I be frightened?"

His expression intent, he studied her. "Perhaps because you've suddenly realized you're getting in too deep?"

She looked away from him, her clasp tightening on the blanket. "I don't love you, Ricardo."

"Don't you? I think you do and just won't admit it. Loving me would disrupt the neat, cozy life you've planned for yourself, and it frightens you. You think that I'll—"

"I don't love you, Ricardo." She interrupted, desperation threading her voice. "Why won't you believe me?"

"I can't believe you. It would hurt too much," he said simply.

Lara could feel the moisture stinging her eyes. "Dammit, you're not being fair. I never asked for any of this."

"I know." He reached out and pulled her into his arms, pushing her cheek into the hollow of his shoulder. "Poor baby." He rocked her back and forth, his arms tightening into a strong haven around her. "That's what you get when you wander away from your safe backyard into the cold world."

The world didn't feel cold with his arms around her and his heart thundering beneath her ear. Neither coldness nor loneliness existed here in Ricardo's embrace. She should back away from him, she thought dreamily. She felt more joined to him now than she had when she had held him within her body.

His lips feathered her temple. "Don't worry, I'll keep you warm. I'll never let you be hurt again."

"You can't keep a promise like that. Everyone's responsible for his own well being," she whispered. "I carry my own burdens."

"Not when there's love. Then responsibility is a privilege, not a burden."

Love, again. Uneasiness stirred within her. "I don't want to talk about—"

"Shh, it's all right." He was rocking her again. "We won't talk about it. You'll just know it's there waiting for you when you're ready. Okay?"

It wasn't okay, she thought. He hadn't accepted that she wouldn't love him. He might never accept it. What if she hurt him more than she had already?

"You're worrying again." He lifted her chin on the crook of his finger to look down into her eyes. "It's okay, I tell you. I'm tough. I can take anything that happens to me."

He was tough, but he was also gentle and exquisitely sensitive to her every thought and emotion. Her throat tightened achingly as she looked up at him. "Sure?"

"Sure." His warm lips tenderly moved back and forth on her own. "But the question is, can you take anything that happens to you?"

She stiffened warily. "What do you mean?"

"Nothing threatening. I just intend to take full advantage of you tonight." His hand left her chin and moved down and twitched away the blanket she had tucked around her breasts. "I didn't want to continue your sexual education with that bastard Jurado listening in and licking his chops." His head lowered and his lips brushed her upper breasts. "There are all sorts of interesting positions that require a little verbal instruction along the way."

Relief rushed through her as she realized he had been speaking of physical not emotional endurance. Lust was fleeting; lust was safe. She smiled and said lightly, "I've always been a good student."

"Wonderful." He jerked the blanket aside as he lowered her to the pallet and then turned her over on her stomach, his hard palms gently squeezing and caressing her bottom. "And it's not that I don't trust your word." His lips caressed the flesh between her shoulder blades as he moved over her, lazily rubbing against her, letting her feel the textures of him, the soft springy hair thatching his chest, the hard cording of muscular thighs, the harder, hotter, length of his arousal. "But suppose we run a few in-depth tests?"

"You've been outside." Lara opened sleepy eyes as Ricardo slipped beneath the blanket onto her pallet and drew her into his arms. He was a dark shape above her, his sable hair gilded by the firelight. He was still dressed, she noticed as she cuddled closer. "I thought you were in the war room with Paco."

"How do you know I went outside?" Ricardo bent down and kissed her temple before raising himself to look down at her, bracing himself with his elbows on either side of her body.

"You smell of wind and leaves." Lara breathed in

the scent of him. "Wonderful. Much nicer than the dank mustiness of the caverns."

He went still. "Being here in the caverns bothers you?"

"Sometimes. I love the sun." She suddenly stiffened. "Why did you go outside? Another raid?"

"No raid. I went to the village of San Esteban. It's about five miles from here." His dark eyes suddenly glinted with mischief. "To see a woman."

"Is that supposed to make me jealous?" A smile tugged at Lara's lips. "You've been keeping me too busy in that line of endeavor to convince me you have to go scavenging the villages for more. Even you don't have that much sexual stamina."

"You obviously haven't been keeping up with my press clippings. I'm reputed to be a superman."

"And are you?"

"No. Just a man." He burrowed his lips in the hollow of her throat. "Except with you. You make me feel like a giant."

Her chest tightened with emotion and she swallowed before she could speak. "Do I?" Her hand reached up to stroke his hair. "That's nice."

He lifted his head. "Aren't you going to ask who I went to see?"

"Why, when you're obviously going to tell me anyway?"

"Rosa Sardona." He threw the blanket aside and sat up. "The wife of the mayor of San Esteban. A lovely lady with exquisite taste."

"I'm happy for her."

Ricardo sighed. "You're an unnatural woman. If not jealousy, haven't you, at least, a spark of curiosity?"

Lara sat up and draped the blanket around her

bare shoulders. She had never seen Ricardo like this. He appeared years younger, full of mischief and boyish eagerness. She smiled indulgently. "Very well, I'm curious. Why did you go to see the lovely Señora Sardona with the exquisite taste?"

"Because I wanted to give you this." He reached behind him and picked up a paper sack beside the pallet. "It wasn't safe for me to go to a shop, but the Sardonas are my people and I didn't think you'd mind—" He thrust the sack at her. "Open it."

She gazed at him in bewilderment and then slowly opened the sack and peered into the bag.

Yellow velvet. Bright as sunlight, soft as night.

She reached into the bag and pulled out an enchanting lemon-yellow robe. She stared in wonder at the garment.

"Stand up."

She got to her feet, and the blanket dropped to a gray pool on the stones. "Lovely," he murmured as he brushed a kiss on the upper slope of her left breast. "Softer than the velvet."

"Why did you go to all this trouble?"

He took the robe and held it while she slipped her arms into the extravagantly wide sleeves. "Because I knew how your hair would shine against the yellow. Sunlight on sunlight." He tied the cord around her waist, lifted her long fair hair free of the collar and tidied it. "There. Now you look like a princess."

"Why, Ricardo?" she asked again.

His smiled faded. "Because I wanted to give you something. God knows, you deserve it. I keep you in a dark cave, away from the sunlight. The food is terrible; there's nothing bright or interesting in your life. I know a secondhand robe isn't much, but I hoped—"

"It's perfectly lovely." She blinked to keep back the tears. "And no one in his right mind can say you're not interesting." She touched the soft velvet of the bodice of the robe. "I love it."

"Truly?" His manner was strangely awkward. "It's the first present I've given anyone for over ten years. My mother liked presents and I thought you might too."

"I do." She whirled in a circle and the full skirt of the velvet robe swirled about her. "I feel very grand. At home I sleep in one of Brett's old T-shirts. I'm afraid I'm not the elegant type that your Señora Sardona must be."

"You're just right." He caught her in his arms and gave here a quick kiss before releasing her. "I brought you something else." He reached down into the paper bag and pulled out a bottle of red wine and two glasses. "For our celebration."

"Celebration?"

"Our one-week anniversary." He handed her a glass, poured wine into it and then his own. "May there be a thousand and one more." He smiled. "I sound like a wishful Scheherazade, don't I?"

She unconsciously tensed. "That's a long time. I believe the *Arabian Nights* tales called for a thousand and one nights, not weeks."

"So I'm greedy." He set the bottle of wine on the floor. "Now, sit down and drink your wine." He pulled her down, cradling her in his arms before the low crackling fire. "And if you're very good, I'll play Scheherazade and tell you a story."

She relaxed back against him. "What kind of story?"

"Whatever you like. You've given me my week; I'd be miserly not to give you whatever you choose." He thought for a moment. "Perhaps not a story. What about a poem?"

"One of yours?"

He shook his head. "Mine all seem to be too dark these days. I've always liked Robert Louis Stevenson. His verse has a certain rough vigor and truth." He quoted softly,

> "Trusty, dusky, vivid, true,
> With eyes of gold and bramble-dew,
> Steel true and blade straight
> The great Artificer made my mate.
>
> Honor, anger, valor, fire,
> A love that life could never tire,
> Death quench, or evil stir,
> The mighty Master gave to her.

She was silent for a long moment before she finally said quietly, "I've never heard that before. It's beautiful."

"It's more. It's you." Before she could speak, he smiled with an effort and said, "You're not drinking your wine. Rosa told me it was a very good year." His lips twisted. "Not that I'd know. I haven't tasted good wine in so long, I can't appreciate the difference. I remember at the rancho my mother used to serve—" He stopped and then lifted his glass to his lips. "Let's drink to better wines and better times next year."

"Maybe next year will be different. You said one more campaign might be all it takes to win your war." She sipped the wine. It was as good as Ricardo said, full-bodied, with a delicate bite. "Perhaps this time next year the war will be over and you can go home to your rancho."

He shook his head. "I don't know if I can."

"What do you mean?"

"I've been a soldier all my adult life. It's all I know. How do I just put down my weapons and start life over?"

"You speak as if you like being a soldier."

"I hate it." He looked down into the ruby depths of his glass. "But it's what I am and I don't know what else I am these days."

"Did you like living on the rancho?"

"Yes, I would never have been the rancher my father was, but I liked the work and the outdoors." He paused. "And the peace. I liked the stillness and the peace."

"Then why couldn't you go back?"

"I've seen too much. When I was a boy, I used to make up poems about sunsets and seas and mountains. Now I can only see the people."

"I don't understand."

"I see pollution in the seas, mountains carved and gouged by miners, sunsets clouded by smog. I can only see the problems, not the beauty. I can't live just for myself any longer." He kissed her ear. "Lord, I wish I could go back to that other time."

"Well, they won't let you. Dr. Salazar says they'll want you to be president."

"Perhaps."

"There's no perhaps about it." She took another sip of wine. "You know how your people feel about you. You're a legend."

"I'm tired of being a legend." Ricardo's hand tightened on his glass. "Maybe I'll run away to your small town and forget Saint Pierre exists."

"You can't do that." She was careful not to look at him. "Paco once told me you *are* Saint Pierre."

"Great." His laugh held a hint of desperation. "Now I'm not only a legend, I'm the whole bloody country."

She tilted her head to look up at him. His mood was strange tonight, alternating between boyish exuberance and despair. He had always been totally mature, possessing an unshakable strength and resolve. Now he was showing her a more human, vulnerable Ricardo Lázaro, and she experienced a sudden rush of tenderness. She mustn't feel like this. Every day they were growing closer, every night more passionate. Where could it end? She deliberately kept her tone light. "Paco said it; I didn't. Personally, I think it sounds a tad uncomfortable being a hero. I wouldn't have it on a bet."

"I know." His lips twisted bitterly. "You only want your little town and your dog and your lake."

"Yes, it's what I want." But if she wanted all that so much, why did the familiar vision seem far way and unsubstantial now? The only reality existed in these caverns with Paco, Manuel, Dr. Salazar, and Ricardo . . . always, Ricardo.

"Have you finished your wine?"

"Yes."

He took her glass and put it with his own on one of the flat stones encircling the fire. "Time for bed."

"The celebration is over?"

He stood up and drew her to her feet. "Oh, no." He started to untie the belt of her robe. "The celebration is just beginning, *querida.*"

Seven

"Ricardo, wait. I can't get my breath." Lara laughed helplessly, trying to match his long stride as Ricardo pulled her through the twisting corridors of the labyrinthlike caverns. "Where are we going?"

"You'll see." Ricardo smiled as he glanced back at her. "A surprise."

"Another one? You do believe in celebrations, don't you?"

"Last night was the celebration that we made it through the week."

"And what is today?"

"The first day of the new week. I thought we should start it right." He rounded a corner. "Outside."

Daylight!

Lara stopped in the path, staring at the clear morning light streaming through the opening at the end of the corridor and illuminating the eternal dimness of the caverns. Exhilaration soared through her.

She hadn't realized how much she had missed the sunlight until this moment. "We're going outside?"

Ricardo's gaze fastened on her face as if he were drinking in her reaction. "You said you missed it."

"I do. But is it safe?"

"For a little while." He pulled her toward the front entrance. "Not for very long. There have been reports of snipers drifting down from the hills since the raid on the Abbey."

She stood in the doorway behind the screen of foliage hiding the entrance of the cave and lifted her face to the sunlight. She sighed blissfully. "Wonderful."

"You look as if you're absorbing it into your pores," Ricardo laughed. "I think you like this better than your velvet robe."

She breathed deeply, taking in the scent of dew-wet leaves, earth, and the orchids growing on the trees in the rain forest a few yards distant. "It's certainly more heady than the wine we drank last night." She glanced anxiously at him. "Are you sure it's safe for you?"

He nodded as he took her hand. "Paco sent three sentries to the lake. If they see any sign of snipers, they'll alert us."

"Lake?"

He grinned. "I can't provide you with your small town or your cottage, but I can give you the lake." He led her away from the entrance of the caverns into the rain forest. "It's only five minutes from here."

The blue of the lake dazzled Lara's eyes. Rimmed by the rain forest, surrounded by the green hills, it shone jewellike in the strong sunlight.

"The waters are warmer than the pool in the caverns. Would you like to swim?" Ricardo asked.

"Could we?"

Ricardo smiled indulgently at her eager expression. "You can. I'll sit here on the bank and watch you."

"You don't want to swim? How can you resist it?" She was quickly shedding her boots and socks even as she spoke. "Real sunlight and that beautiful water."

He dropped down on the mossy bank. "Leave your shirt on. We don't want to give the sentries a free show."

Lara glanced around her as she stepped out of her trousers. "I don't see them."

"You're not supposed to see them. Take my word for it; they're there."

She ran toward the lake, shirttails flapping about her thighs. She dived into the lake, cleaving the water arrow-straight, and then set out with a strong breaststroke across the lake.

The water was comfortably cool, deliciously silky against her flesh.

"Not too far," Ricardo called.

She reluctantly turned and began swimming back toward him. "I could go on forever," she shouted exultantly. "Oh, Ricardo, thank you."

A shadow crossed his face. "You're easily pleased."

"What do you mean? My own private lake, sunshine, orchids growing on the trees." She felt for the bottom with a tentative foot, located it, and stood upright. She shook her wet hair back from her face. "I *love* it."

"I can see that you do." Ricardo smiled at her, his eyes narrowed against the glare of the sunlight on the water.

He was so beautiful.

Lara stood in the shoulder-high water and just looked at him. His arms were linked about his knees in the position she knew so well. He was the intense, controlled man she had known in the cell; the boyish, vulnerable lover of last night; the poet-warrior. Suddenly, as she looked at him, everything he was merged for her, sweeping away doubts and choices, overwhelming everything but the one truth she had been fighting for so long.

Dear God, she loved him.

"Lara?" Ricardo's gaze was intent on her face, the muscles of his body stiffening as he saw her expression.

What a time for such a monumental truth to strike home—up to her neck in cold water and Ricardo yards away on the bank. She started toward him, trying to move swiftly through the heavy water that was keeping her from him.

By the time she reached the bank, he was standing at the edge holding out his hand. He pulled her up to stand beside him.

The wet shirt clung to her body, but she scarcely felt the chill as both of Ricardo's hands cupped her cheeks. He looked down into her eyes. "Yes?" he whispered.

She couldn't speak; she couldn't do anything but look at him and wonder how she had come to this point of no return.

Joy illuminated his features as his head bent slowly toward her. "*Querida*, it's what you—"

A sharp crack!

Ricardo jerked.

Blood stained the upper left side of his shirt and—

"Down!" Ricardo shoved her into the shrubbery a

few yards away, pushed her to the ground, and dived on top of her.

It had been a shot!

Ricardo had been shot! He was bleeding.

Panic caused Lara's breath to stop as she finally realized what had happened. A sniper had fired from one of the trees in the rain forest. "Let me up. You're hurt."

"Stay still." He held her immobile, his body heavy on hers, pinning her to the ground. "He's still out there."

More shots.

She couldn't tell where the shots were coming from or at whom they were aimed. Ricardo was covering her with his body. For all she knew, those bullets could be tearing into his flesh. "No!" She fought him wildly, managing to slip from beneath his bulk and onto her knees. One glance told her he probably hadn't been hit more than the one time, but she had no idea how bad the wound was. "We've got to get you back to the cave."

"Wait!" His hand fell on her shoulder, keeping her on her knees. "We don't even know if there was more than one sniper."

"I don't care." The tears were running down her cheeks. "You're probably bleeding to death, dammit."

"I don't think it hit an artery, and the bullet passed through." Ricardo paled with sudden shock and he went rigid. "It passed right through my shoulder," he repeated dully.

She scarcely heard him as she quickly unbuttoned his shirt. "We shouldn't have come out of the caverns. I shouldn't have let you—"

"Ricardo!" Paco stood beside them, his face almost

as pale as Ricardo's. "Dammit, I told you it was a risk." He knelt beside them on the ground. "Bad?"

"Nothing." Ricardo pushed Lara's hands aside and rose to his knees. "Did they get them?"

Paco nodded. "Sniper, working alone. Let's get you back to the caverns so Juan can clean up that wound." He helped Ricardo to his feet, sliding a protective arm about his waist. "*Dios*, you're stupid. The most-wanted man on Saint Pierre and you have to go swimming." He shook his head. "In broad daylight."

He hadn't gone swimming, Lara thought. He had sat on the bank and watched her, guarded her, because he had known how great the danger was.

"Shut up, Paco," Ricardo said wearily. "You don't have to tell me how stupid I am. It has just been brought home to me in the most effective way possible." He didn't look at Lara as he let Paco half carry him down the path through the rain forest. "Get dressed, Lara. I'll send one of the men to bring you back to the caverns. Stay where you are until he comes for you."

"But I want to go with you."

He didn't answer and in a moment he had disappeared behind the thick screen of shrubbery of the rain forest.

She stared after him in bewilderment, feeling isolated, shut out, terribly alone.

Lara hurried into her clothes but had to wait another few minutes for the sentry to arrive to take her back to the caverns. By the time she reached the infirmary, Paco was nowhere in sight. Salazar had finished bandaging Ricardo's shoulder, and Manuel was handing him a clean shirt to slip on.

"Are you okay?" Lara hurried toward him across the room. "Is he okay, Juan?"

Juan Salazar nodded. "Fine. The shoulder will be stiff for a day or two, but it was scarcely worth a bandage."

"It bled—" Lara shuddered as she stopped before Ricardo. "You're certain?"

"I've had much worse wounds." Ricardo slid his arms awkwardly into the shirt and started to button it. His lips twisted grimly. "But none I've deserved more."

"No one deserves to be shot. Here, let me help you with that." She reached out to button his shirt.

"No!" He took a step back away from her. "I don't need help. I'm fine."

"You've just been shot. That's not fine. I want to help you, dammit."

For an instant something flickered beneath the expressionless mask he had assumed. "I know you do." His gaze dropped to the fastenings of the shirt he was buttoning. "Go to your quarters. I have to talk to Paco about the sniper. I'll join you when I've finished with him."

She was dismissed. This was not the Ricardo she knew. She might as well have been one of the soldiers in his command. This man was crisp, commanding, coolly remote.

She hesitated, staring at him uncertainly. She could sense the doctor's discomfort as he gazed at both of them, but she ignored him as she asked urgently, "Ricardo, what's wrong?"

"Nothing." He didn't look at her again as he strode from the infirmary.

She turned immediately to Salazar. "Are you sure there's nothing seriously wrong with him? I've never seen him like this before."

"You've seen Ricardo, the general, for the first time." Salazar grimaced. "I told you he could be intimidating."

"Yes." Her tone was abstracted as she turned and moved toward the door. Everything would be all right, she assured herself. She couldn't expect Ricardo to behave normally. He had just been shot, for heaven's sake. Probably by the time he finished his talk with Paco and came to her quarters, he'd be entirely himself again.

Ricardo's manner was exactly the same when he walked into her room two hours later—remote, cool, completely impersonal.

"Paco interrogated the sniper. The location of the caverns hasn't been compromised."

"That's good." Lara's fingers nervously laced together as she leaned back against the stone wall. "Will the junta send someone else when he doesn't report in?"

"Probably. But not for a day or two. We have time to get you out."

She froze. "What?"

"I've told Paco to radio for a helicopter to take you to Barbados."

She stared at him without speaking.

"The helicopter will arrive on the island shortly after dark. Be ready."

"Why?" she whispered.

"It's best."

She rose jerkily to her feet. "What do you mean

'it's best'? Who the devil is it best for, and why are you acting like a damn robot?"

"I'm not acting like a robot. I'm behaving like a responsible commander." His lips twisted. "At last. I'm not surprised you don't recognize it. I haven't exhibited anything but blatant self-indulgence since I brought you here. I let my sex drive get in the way of my good sense. After five months in prison I suppose it would have been excusable in someone who didn't have a revolution to run but not—"

"Sex? You're saying I wasn't anything more to you than a good lay?" She shook her head. "I don't believe you."

"Why not? You told me yourself it was no more than that."

"But that was before—" She stopped. That was before she had realized he was the center of her existence, before she had discovered that she loved him. Why did the fact that she loved him have to mean he still loved her? Few things came out evenly in this world. "You said you loved me."

"I was wrong. I mistook gratitude and sex for something else." He shrugged. "I've gone through nine years of madness; I suppose I was reaching out for something sane and real."

The words were cutting into her with agonizing sharpness. "May I ask what brought this sudden rush of responsibility to the forefront?"

"A bullet through the shoulder is an excellent reminder of duty. Another inch or so and I would have been dead."

She shuddered as she remembered that moment when she had seen the blood flowing from the wound. "Yes."

"And, though I don't believe I'm as important to

the revolution as Paco says, my death would be a
definite setback now that we have victory within our
grasp." He shook his head in self-disgust. "And I
risked all we've fought to gain for the last nine years
just to let you take a sunbath."

"I wouldn't have let you do it if I'd known." Lara
could barely get the words past her lips. She
wouldn't cry. She wouldn't let him see the pain. "I
didn't want any of this to happen."

"It did happen." Ricardo stared at the craggy wall
past her left shoulder. "You'd better get something
to eat before you leave. It's a long flight."

Food. He was talking about food? "Haven't you
forgotten something?"

"I don't think so."

"What if I'm pregnant? Wasn't that why you
insisted I stay in the beginning?"

He flinched, his gaze shifting to her face. "Naturally, I'm concerned," he said haltingly. "I'll expect
you to let me know if that happens."

"The hell I will." A jolt of anger momentarily banished the pain. "I told you once it would be my child.
I won't come running and give you the choice of
whether you want to bear the burden. No, thank
you."

"It's my responsibility to care—"

"The hell with your responsibility. I've had it with
your—" She broke off and shook her head dazedly.
This was all wrong. It couldn't be happening. She
had been so sure in that moment by the lake. She
looked up and said carefully, "You have to be lying.
It wasn't only sex. I know it."

"No, you're right. It was a dream, but it's time I
woke from that dream." He smiled sadly. "It was
also nostalgia. You're a very special woman and you

reminded me of the old life. You brought back a beautiful memory, Lara, and I thank you for it."

When she remembered the conversation of last night, his words sounded reasonable. Why couldn't she have realized earlier that she loved him? Perhaps she could have turned her longing for the past into something more. Now it was too late. "You're welcome." Her tone was brittle. "Any time."

"The helicopter will land in a glade near the caverns. I'll send Paco to get you an hour before it's due to arrive." He hesitated. "You've given us so much, but there's one more favor I'm going to ask of you. Manuel. Will you take him with you? When we launch the offensive, it won't be safe for him here. I promise I'll send for him as soon as the war is over and pay his expenses while he's in Barbados with—"

"Of course I'll take him," she interrupted harshly. "But I won't take your money."

He nodded and turned toward the door. "Goodbye, Lara."

"Wait."

He looked back over his shoulder.

"Say it," she said desperately. "I have to hear you say it. Look me in the eye and tell me you don't love me."

He was silent a long moment and then he turned to face her. He stared directly into her eyes and said slowly, enunciating every word clearly, "I don't love you, Lara."

She closed her eyes tightly as the pain rushed through her.

She heard him mutter something under his breath, and then she heard his footsteps echoing on the stone as he left her quarters.

*   *   *

The beige and red helicopter hovered over the ground and touched down on the grass.

Manuel started at a run across the glade while Paco and Lara moved at a slower pace.

Paco frowned. "I don't like to see you go like this."

Lara looked straight ahead at the helicopter. "Ricardo was right. I don't have a place here."

"You belong to us now. Ricardo's not thinking straight."

"He appears to be perfectly lucid."

They had reached the helicopter and Paco opened the passenger door and Manuel scrambled into the rear seat.

"Forgive him, Lara," Paco said softly.

"You forgive him. He's your friend."

"And what is he to you?"

"An episode." She tried to smile at him. "An adventure that's now at an end."

Paco shook his head.

"Don't look so sad. None of this is your fault." She leaned forward and kissed his cheek. "Good-bye, Paco. Take care of yourself."

"And you." Paco lifted her into the helicopter, his dark eyes shining in the glare of the helicopter's landing lights. "*Vaya con Dios*, Lara."

He slammed the heavy door and ducked back away from the spinning rotors.

Lara heard a murmur from Manuel in the back-seat and she turned to see him staring at Paco with tear-bright eyes.

"It won't be for long," Lara said. "You'll be able to come home soon, Manuel."

"I know." His voice was husky as he wiped his eyes on the back of his hand. "I'm a soldier and a soldier does what he's ordered to do. I'm not crying. Dust got in my eyes."

"I see." Lara could feel a hot stinging behind her own lids as she looked at Paco through the window. It seemed such a short time since she had first walked into Paco's command tent weeks before, and yet those minutes had changed her entire world.

The pilot started the engine and a moment later the helicopter lifted off, soaring high above the trees, before turning toward Barbados.

When Lara walked into Brett's hospital room the next afternoon, he was sitting in his wheelchair by the window. As she looked at him, she felt a rush of relief that temporarily lifted her mood. Brett's color was good and he appeared stronger than when Lara had seen him less than a month before.

"I should break your neck," he said as she bent down to brush a kiss on his cheek. "I nearly went into a tailspin when your note was delivered the day after you left for Saint Pierre. You had no business going there."

"You're my business." She sat down on the visitor's chair next to the table by the window. "You're looking well. Have you started therapy?"

"Last week." He grimaced. "It couldn't have been this hard learning to walk when I was an infant. You'd think I'd do it better now."

"You'll get there."

"Stop making encouraging noises and tell me what happened on Saint Pierre."

"Nothing very interesting. Lázaro is free."

"I know. I heard about his escape from the Abbey. Were you involved?"

"In a small way." She changed the subject. "When do you get to go home?"

"The doctor said he'd like me to stick around Barbados until my initial therapy is finished." He met her gaze. "But I'm not going back to the United States, Lara."

Her hand tightened on her purse. "Saint Pierre?"

He nodded. "I found something there."

She smiled crookedly. "The Pied Piper."

"He's a remarkable man."

"Yes." She avoided his glance. "You know the war will probably be over by the time you're on your feet again? Paco says one more campaign should do it."

"I'll still go back." Brett reached over to cover her hand with his own. "Come with me, Lara. Saint Pierre's going to be a new frontier, a new world."

She shook her head. "You and Lázaro are the empire builders. I'm Betsy Ross who sits by the fire and sews the flag."

"That's not what Paco says."

Her eyes lifted swiftly to his face. "Paco?"

"He radioed a message to me when you left Saint Pierre with explicit orders from Ricardo." A smile tugged at his lips. "You must have done some valuable work down there. Paco says you're a national heroine."

"He exaggerates."

"Ricardo's orders are that my sole duty until further notice is to take care of you."

She felt the color rise in her cheeks. "I can take care of myself. How did you get the message?"

"Ricardo has several men stationed here in Barbados. They funnel supplies and send information from the outside world."

"Did Paco tell you I brought Manuel back with me?"

He nodded. "I'm surprised the boy came. He's nuts about Ricardo."

"He's only nine years old and he thinks he's a soldier who has to obey orders. He's infected with the same war hysteria as the rest of you." She shook her head. "I'm beginning to think the male of the species is a little mad. You, in particular, brother dear."

"You always did." Brett squeezed her hand. "You never let yourself see that you were exactly like me. You'd go crazy without an occasional challenge."

She shook her head. "You're wrong. I like the quiet life."

"Am I wrong? Did you really go down to Saint Pierre because you wanted to keep me from going back or because you were jealous?"

She stared at him, dumbfounded. "Jealous?"

"We've always been able to telegraph our thoughts and feelings to each other since we were kids. I talked a hell of a lot about Lázaro and Saint Pierre. Didn't you really want to see and taste for yourself what I had found down there?"

"No, it's not true. I didn't—" She stopped. Both Paco and Ricardo had said she didn't really know herself and she had adapted to life in the caverns with astonishing speed. Had she been lying to herself all these years?

"Think about returning to Saint Pierre with me. I don't want to lose you." He opened the drawer in the bedside table. "Do me a favor?"

"What?"

"Read this." He pulled out a slim volume and handed it to her.

Right to Choose, by Ricardo Lázaro.

She automatically flinched. "No."

"A favor," Brett repeated softly.

"It wouldn't do any good. I can't go back to Saint Pierre, Brett. There's nothing there for me."

"Read the book."

She blindly took the book and thrust it into her canvas bag. "I have to go. I've rented a small apartment near the hospital and Manuel is waiting for me." She smiled brightly. "We have to go shopping. Manuel and I are both practically naked. Combat gear just doesn't cut it in the big city."

"How are you fixed for money?"

"Well enough. I'll worry about your medical bills later."

"Ricardo will take care of them. The revolution is very well funded now, and the hospital bills for all his men in Barbados are sent to his backers in Europe and the United States."

"That's good to know." Lara stood up and leaned down to press a quick kiss on the top of his blond hair. "I'll be back tomorrow."

"Late in the afternoon. I have my therapy in the morning and I growl at everyone for at least two hours afterward."

"I can take it."

He stared at her appraisingly before he nodded slowly. "Yes, I think you can. You're a lot tougher than before you went to Saint Pierre."

"Maybe." She turned and walked toward the door. "I'll see you tomorrow."

"Promise me you'll read the book."

"Lord, you're stubborn." She gave him an exasperated glance over her shoulder. "All right, I'll read the blasted book."

"Soon?"

She sighed. "Soon."

He grinned. "And you'll tell me what happened on Saint Pierre that made Paco say you were a national heroine?"

"Someday, maybe."

"Well, you win some, you lose some."

Yes, you did, and at the moment Lara felt she had lost more than she had won on Saint Pierre.

The heavy door of the hospital room swung shut behind her.

Two weeks later Ricardo Lázaro launched an offensive against the junta. Within four days the junta's forces were in retreat and two days later the *palacio* was taken.

From the balcony of the *palacio* Ricardo announced the surrender of the junta, the establishment of the Republic of Saint Pierre, and the first democratic elections to be held on the island in over twenty years.

Three weeks later Ricardo Lázaro was elected by a landslide as president of the Republic of Saint Pierre.

Brett wistfully looked up from the newspaper. "Damn, I'd like to be there for the inauguration."

"Maybe you will be," Lara said. "You're on crutches now and I'm sure you'll be on the A-list for an invitation."

"So will you." Brett grinned. "Paco wouldn't dare not issue an invitation to a 'national heroine,' would he?"

Lara shook her head. "I won't be invited."

"Sure you will." Brett's voice grew coaxing. "And wouldn't you like to go to the inaugural ball with the crème de la crème? According to this article, you'd be elbow to elbow with every head-of-state in the world."

"Then they can do without this humble head," Lara said. "And, speaking of heads, I have to go. I have an appointment at three to have the hair on this lowly head trimmed."

"Have you read the book?"

He asked the question every time she came to see him, and her reply was always the same. "Not yet." She held up her hand as he opened his lips. "Soon."

He nodded. "How is Manuel?"

"Very good but aching to get back to Saint Pierre. I thought he'd enjoy a taste of movies and television and all the rest of the things kids like, but he looks down his nose at them. It's really sad." She shook her head. "He's forgotten how to be a little boy."

"Ricardo should send for him soon."

"Yes, and I'll miss him."

"You'd better go or you'll be late for your appointment." When she didn't immediately rise from her chair, Brett looked at her speculatively. "You don't seem very eager. Don't you want to go?"

She didn't know how she felt about this appointment that she had just lied to Brett about. Her emotions were in a tumult. One moment she was frightened, the next excited.

"Of course." She smiled with an effort as she rose to her feet. "Yes, you're right. I'd better go."

Eight

"Seven months. June." Dr. Cambrian's white smile lit her dusky face. "You're in very good health and should have an entirely normal birth."

"You're sure?" Lara moistened her lips with her tongue. "June."

"Quite sure." The doctor's British accent resounded in the affirmative. "I'll prescribe iron tablets and I want to see you again next month."

"I may not be here next month. I'm planning on going back to the States."

"You're unmarried?" the doctor asked. "It's not good to be alone at a time like this. Do you have friends in the United States?"

"Yes." Lara rose to her feet. "I'll be fine. Thank you, Dr. Cambrian, you've been very kind. If I'm still in Barbados next month, I'll be sure to make an appointment."

A few minutes later Lara was out on the street, walking toward her apartment building a few blocks away.

A baby. What would she do with a baby? She still had to start her career. Now she would have to worry about baby-sitters and supporting two instead of one—

A baby.

Joy suddenly burst through her with dazzling strength, catching her off guard. A miracle, a child to love. All the problems that had loomed so large faded into insignificance before the knowledge of the gift she had been given. She could work out the difficulties. She was strong and healthy and fairly intelligent. Why had she been so worried?

Manuel was sitting curled up in a chair reading when she entered the apartment. He had discovered the public library the first week he had arrived in Barbados and had been devouring books ever since. He was dressed in jeans, T-shirt, and tennis shoes, and the clothes somehow looked inappropriate on him. The clothes were young; the eyes he lifted from his book were old. "Your brother is well?"

"Wonderful." She tossed her purse on the couch. "Everything is wonderful."

He smiled. "That is good." He hesitated. "And Dr. Cambrian says you are well too?"

She turned to look at him. "How did you know I went to the doctor today?"

"I saw the name and the appointment on the note you left on the telephone table. I was worried."

"Oh, it was nothing. I'm getting some vitamin tablets to make me feel better."

Manuel put the book on the table and studied her. "You look happy."

"Yes." Lara ran across the room and gave him a quick hug. "I'm happy and healthy and I think we should celebrate. Let's go out to dinner. I passed a little restaurant down the street and the smells wafting through those doors were delicious."

"I'd like that." His tone was grave. "But I must return these books to the library." He stood up and gathered the pile of books on the table into his arms. "I'll be back in two hours." He moved toward the door. "Now you should rest, I think."

As the door closed behind him, she shook her head bemusedly. Would Manuel ever get over that heavy sense of responsibility? Another child wouldn't have thought twice about letting books run a day overdue, and yet Manuel had stopped reading in mid story to make sure he got the book back in time. She had grown even more fond of Manuel in these last weeks and she would miss him terribly when Ricardo sent for him.

But she would soon have a child of her own.

Not only her own but Ricardo's.

Her smile faded as she realized that a good portion of the joy she was experiencing was because this was Ricardo's child. Dear heaven, she had hoped she was getting over him, but there was a terrible sweetness in the knowledge that she would now always have a part of Ricardo with her.

The baby would be part of Ricardo and yet the child would receive only a genetic legacy from him. In a few weeks Lara would return to the United States, and Ricardo would be out of her life. What could she tell her child about its father when she had barely known him herself? She had known the lover and the prisoner in the cell. She knew little about the man the rest of the world knew.

She rose to her feet and moved slowly to the closet across the room. Ricardo's book was still in the canvas tote bag on the shelf where she had placed it the afternoon Brett had given it to her. She took the slim volume out of the bag and carried it back to the couch. She sat down and opened the book to the first page.

Two hours later she closed the book and leaned her head back against the cushions of the couch. Her throat was tight with tears, yet she felt exhilarated.

She had been wrong. Her child had a legacy. Dear God, what a legacy Ricardo had left the world in this book. Gradually, as she had read, all the bitterness and hurt she had felt toward Ricardo had disappeared. The book was written without self-pity, and yet the suffering and loneliness of the years resounded in every word. If their time together had eased both his loneliness and her own, what right had she to demand he give her more?

The man who had written this book was an extraordinary human being as well as a patriot. Even if he wasn't able to love her, he was a man well worth loving. He had told her once he had wanted to write words that would shake the world, and these words had shaken and stirred her to the depths. She now knew why Brett had gone to Saint Pierre to fight.

"I'm back." Manuel threw open the door and ran into the apartment. "Now we can go—what's wrong?"

"Nothing."

"You've been crying." His eyes searched her face. "Why have—" He saw the book and nodded, relieved. "Oh, it's okay, then."

"Is it?"

"You needn't be ashamed. I've seen soldiers cry when reading Ricardo's book," he said matter-of-factly. "You scared me. I thought you were sick." He took the book away from her and put it on the table by the couch. "Now we can go to the restaurant. Then I think you should come home and rest."

She lifted her brows. "Why are you so set on my resting? I told you I was fine."

"I have to take—" He stopped and smiled at her. "You would not have gone to the doctor if you had felt entirely well." He tugged at her hand to pull her to her feet. "Come on. Now we eat."

Lara stirred from a deep sleep.

A sound . . .

She opened drowsy eyes and saw a shadowy face bending over her. Fear jarred her into full wakefulness. She opened her lips to scream.

A hand clapped over her mouth. "Shh, it's all right. It's me, Paco."

"Paco!" Lara's eyes widened with shock as she twisted her head to avoid Paco's hard, callused hand. "You scared me to death." She reached over and turned on the lamp on the bedside table. The resulting pool of light revealed a strange, yet familiar, Paco. The same elfin features and bright eyes were there, but Paco wasn't wearing his usual combat gear. He had on a dark-green uniform, with a knifelike crease in the trousers; his jacket sported a full complement of medals. "You look very grand. What are you doing here in the middle of the night?" Before he could speak, she asked, "You've come for Manuel?"

"Yes."

She sat up in bed, pulling up the thin straps of her nightgown that had fallen from her shoulders. "I was afraid of that." She glanced at the clock. "Good heavens, it's three o'clock. Couldn't you have waited until morning? I'll have to go wake him up."

"He's awake and dressed. He let us into the apartment."

"Us?"

"I have a few men in the living room waiting." He paused. "Bodyguards."

She laughed uneasily. "I thought the war was over. You have to travel with bodyguards?"

"Not me."

She looked at him, frowning. "Manuel?"

"No." He grimaced. "You."

"Me?" She swung her feet to the floor. "What the devil are you talking about?"

"Ricardo sent me to bring you back to Saint Pierre."

She felt as if she had been struck in the stomach. "What?"

"He wants to see you."

She felt a sudden soaring of hope and tried desperately to crush it down. "I find that hard to believe. He sent me away."

"Things have changed."

"Not between us."

"Yes," Paco said softly. "Ricardo knows about the child."

Another shock. "He couldn't know—I just found out myself two days ago. How?"

"Manuel."

She looked at him uncomprehendingly.

He shrugged. "Ricardo gave Manuel orders to care for you and report to us regularly. I gave Manuel the name and address of our contact here in Barbados. When he found out you'd gone to a doctor, he let the contact know. That man then called the doctor's office and found out she was an obstetrician and gynecologist."

"You're joking. You're saying Ricardo had Manuel spying on me?" She laughed shakily. "He's only nine years old."

"Ricardo put it to Manuel as protecting and caring for you. It made Manuel's stay easier to know he had a task to do. He's been a soldier for too long to shake—"

"Stop saying that. He's not a soldier. He's only a little— Why am I arguing with you?" She picked up her robe from the chair beside the bed and put it on. "It's all nonsense. I'll make you and your 'body-guards' coffee before you take Manuel."

He shook his head. "You have to come with us."

"The hell I do." She turned on him fiercely. "This child has nothing to do with Ricardo. I'm going back to the States in two weeks and I'll be out of his life for good."

"You don't understand." Steel had entered Paco's voice. "I have orders to bring you back, and I have to do it, Lara."

She looked at him in astonishment. "Are you talking force."

He didn't answer.

"Dear heaven, you'd actually kidnap me?"

"I have a plane waiting at—"

"And what if I struggle? Aren't you afraid of hurting the great liberator's child?"

"We'd see that you didn't hurt yourself." Paco looked both unhappy and uncomfortable. "Manuel said you were happy about the baby. I don't think you'd risk losing it."

"No, by God, I won't let anything happen to—" She stopped. "You're really going to do this thing?"

"I'll have your bags packed while you get dressed."

"I can't believe this."

"He only wants to talk to you, Lara."

"Well, I don't want to talk to him." She hugged herself, trying to still the shivers running through her. She didn't want to see Ricardo and chance being thrown into that chaos of emotions again. In the last two days she had come to terms with her life and her future without him. "We said all we had to say."

"It's his child."

"It's *my* child."

"Then come with us and tell him so."

"I will." She turned and strode toward the bathroom. "Since he doesn't appear to be giving me any choice. I read his book. He doesn't live by his convictions, does he?"

"I think he feels he has no choice himself, this time, Lara."

"He told me once there are always choices. Well, I'm about to give him one or two that he won't find pleasant." She glanced at Paco over her shoulder. "What about Brett? I won't have him sitting in the hospital worrying about me."

"I'll make sure Brett knows about this."

"Not about the child."

Paco shook his head. "I'll tell him we had a very good reason for inviting you back to Saint Pierre."

"Inviting?" She slammed the bathroom door behind her.

* * *

A long black limousine bearing the green, white, and scarlet flag of the Republic of Saint Pierre was waiting by the hangar when the private jet landed shortly before noon.

Paco got into the front seat beside the driver. Manuel clambered into the backseat of the limousine beside Lara. The boy had stayed at Paco's side and scarcely glanced at Lara during the entire flight from Barbados. He didn't look at her now but fastened his eyes on the back of Paco's head as the limousine glided away from the hangar and through the tall wire fence that bordered the landing field. His dark eyes shone moistly in his thin face. "You're angry with me."

"Shouldn't I be? I thought we were friends."

"We are friends. But Ricardo is—"

"The Pied Piper," Lara finished wearily. "Never mind. I'm not really angry with you. I should have known I couldn't expect loyalty from Ricardo's—"

"I *am* loyal to you," Manuel broke in fiercely. "You don't understand. Ricardo said you must be protected."

"From myself?"

"You belong to Ricardo." Manuel's jaw set stubbornly. "He knows what is best for you."

"Manuel, my boy, you've been living in those caves too long. I'm the only one who knows what's best for me."

The limousine glided down the ramp into the street, and Lara glimpsed the massive crenelated stone bulk of the *palacio* on the third hill in the distance. She unconsciously tensed as she thought of the battle that waited for her there.

A small hand crept closer and covered her own on the seat. "Don't be scared," Manuel said. "Paco says he's not angry with you."

"Well, I'm angry with him."

Manuel was silent a moment and then said haltingly, "It was the baby. That was why I did it."

"What?"

"Bad things happen to babies when they're not protected."

And who should know that better than Manuel? she thought with a pang of sadness. Her annoyance with him subsided and she turned her hand over and clasped his. "I'll protect my baby."

"Ricardo can do it better. Ricardo took care of me." He moistened his lips. "I get scared sometimes and I need—Ricardo makes it go away."

It had taken a great deal for Manuel to admit to fear and he had done it as a silent apology for his part in bringing her here against her will. Lara gently touched his mop of dark hair. "Don't worry; whatever happens, I'm not going to blame you."

The limousine drove through the arched gates and across the enormous mosaic-tiled courtyard before stopping in front of the *palacio*.

Two uniformed guards sprang forward to open the passenger doors. Paco got out and stood waiting on the steps until Lara and Manuel joined him.

"Ricardo is in his quarters waiting for you." Paco took Lara's elbow and propelled her into the gleaming foyer. "He apologizes for not meeting you at the airport, but he can't go out on the streets these days without being mobbed and he didn't want to call attention to your arrival."

"Why not? I doubt if anyone would believe the great man capable of kidnapping." Lara glanced around the huge reception area and then up at the frescoes on the ceiling. "This looks like a cathedral. A temple for the great liberator?"

Paco ignored the remark as he looked down at Manuel and they started up the great curving staircase. "The inauguration is tomorrow and we're going to have to get you a fine outfit to wear at the ceremony."

"A uniform like yours?" Manuel asked eagerly.

"We'll see." Paco released Lara's arm as they reached a carved mahogany door guarded by two uniformed soldiers. "Suppose we go to the tailor now and see what he can do for you." He motioned to one of the guards, who immediately threw open the door. "You and I will see Ricardo later, eh?"

Manuel glanced at Lara and then nodded. "Later."

Lara was rigid with tension as she moved toward the open door.

"He's doing what he thinks is right, Lara," Paco said in a low voice, taking Manuel's hand and turning away.

She scarcely heard him as she walked into the sitting room.

Ricardo was standing by the long French window across the room. He was bathed in sunlight that revealed the luster of his dark hair and the tension of his squared shoulders beneath the jacket of his dark-green dress uniform.

She stared at him and suddenly she was feeling the same overwhelming wave of emotion she had experienced that last day at the lake before he had sent her away. She had thought she had come to terms with the past, but it was sweeping back. Dear Lord, she didn't want to feel like this. She didn't want to love him. She groped desperately for the anger and frustration she had felt on the journey here.

She moved forward and stood before him. "You used a child to spy on me. That's despicable, Ricardo."

"Yes, it is," Ricardo agreed quietly. "Despicable. But I could see no other way. You wouldn't have told me about the child."

"No." Lara glared up at him. "You're damn right I wouldn't. I said when we parted that I wouldn't coming running to you if I found I was pregnant."

"Running?" His lips twisted and he shook his head. "I knew you'd have to be roped and tied before you'd accept my help."

"So you sent Paco and your goon squad to drag me back."

He flinched. "They aren't a goon squad. They're your bodyguards. I had to make sure you were safe."

"And wouldn't resist your invitation." Her lips tightened. "I'm here. Say what you want to say and then send me back to Barbados."

"I can't send you back to Barbados. You're carrying my child."

Her eyes widened in disbelief. "So I'm supposed to stay here and let you take care of me? I don't suppose we're talking about marriage?"

"No."

It was the answer she had expected and still the pain spiraled through her. She had to fight desperately to keep him from seeing it.

"I didn't think so." She turned away and looked through the window down into the courtyard. "Then what are you suggesting?" She pretended to think. "Let's see, you want to marry me to one of your officers so that you can keep an eye on your offspring?"

"No." His voice was hoarse and so low she could barely hear it.

"That's good," she said sarcastically. "I'd be disappointed in your lack of ingenuity. That kind of arrangement went out of fashion in the nineteenth century and you're a man of the future, a man who carves new frontiers and—"

"Shut up!" His tone held such violence, her gaze flew to his face. Lines of pain carved either side of his mouth, and his eyes glittered with torment. "I can't take any more of this."

"Why not? Everything I've said is true. What did you have in mind? Perhaps I'm to become *el presidente's* mistress with a covey of bastards clinging to my skirts?"

"No, you can't stay here on Saint Pierre."

"You're probably right. I've noticed you become bored quite easily and it would prove an inconvenience to you to have me—"

His hand clamped over her mouth. It was shaking. His voice also shook as he said, "I told you I couldn't—you're tearing me apart. I know I hurt you. I know I'm hurting you now. But I can't stand here and let you do it to me anymore. It's worse than Jurado's sharp little ice pick jabbing and jabbing and . . ." His hand moved yearningly from her lips to hover above the soft swing of hair touching her shoulders. "Lord, I've wanted to touch you. Do you know how often I've thought of the way you move beneath me and the way you look and smell and . . ." He trailed off and closed his eyes for an instant. Then his lids flicked open and he took a step back. "I'm sorry. I didn't mean to do that."

She gazed at him in wonder, as a tiny glow of hope suddenly flaring within her. Something was wrong here. Or perhaps something was wonderfully right. "Then why did you do it?"

"I couldn't stop—" He broke off and then said jerkily, "What else? Sex rearing its head again. We've always had a very combustible reaction to each other."

He was lying. Oh, there had definitely been lust in his expression, but there had also been something else. The hope flared higher.

She moved away from the French window and dropped into a high-backed cushioned chair. She must be careful. The flame of hope could be infinitely fragile. "Very well, I'm listening. Why am I here?"

"Two reasons. We have to come to an agreement about the child."

"And the other reason?"

"To receive your medal."

She blinked. "For having your child?"

He smiled for the first time since she had entered the room. "I hope the conception wasn't that terrible." His smile faded. "For bravery. Do you still have those whip marks on your back?"

"They're almost gone." She shook her head to clear it. His last words had taken her completely by surprise. "You brought me here to give me a medal?"

"You deserve it. It will be presented tomorrow night at the inauguration ball. The Saint Pierre Ribbon of Courage."

"I don't want a medal."

"You'll receive it anyway." Ricardo's jaw tightened stubbornly. "You gave to us. Now we give to you."

She smiled faintly. "I've already been advised there's a gift on the way."

Ricardo's expression became shadowed. "That's not a gift; it's a burden."

She shook her head and repeated softly, "A gift."

His eyes met hers and suddenly there was a velvet intimacy charging the atmosphere between them. Ricardo tore his gaze away from her and said huskily, "I'm glad you view it in that light, but there are still problems."

"None I can't overcome."

"With my help. I intend to settle enough on you to make you and the child secure for the rest of your lives." He waved his hand as she started to speak. "And I'll assign a man to guard you and the child. You needn't worry. He'll be very unobtrusive."

"Guard me? Why should I need guards?"

"I still have enemies. If they can't get to me, they may try to hurt the people I care about. Even though we'll make sure no one knows that we were lov— close, I'd still feel better if you were protected."

Something that had been tugging at her memory clicked into place. "Protected . . ." She studied him thoughtfully. "Oh, would you?"

"Yes." Ricardo stood with his hands clasped behind his back, his legs astride. "Here's what I plan on doing. Tomorrow night you'll receive your medal. Naturally, we'll be careful not to let anyone know that we are more than friends."

"Naturally."

"The next morning Paco will escort you back to the United States and find you a house wherever you choose."

"By a lake," she murmured.

"If you wish." He frowned. "I know you prefer a small town, but you'll have to be close to good medical care."

"I'm sure Paco can find something that meets the requirements. Do you suppose he can also locate a suitable dog?"

"You're laughing at me."

"At least I'm no longer contemplating flushing your medal down the nearest toilet."

"You'll accept the medal?"

She rose to her feet. "Yes, I believe I'll accept your Ribbon of Courage."

"And the house and—"

"We'll discuss that later. I'll take it under advisement. Now, may I go to my room?" She glanced around the stiff grandeur of the sitting room. "I gather you don't want me here."

Something flickered in his eyes. "Would you stay if I asked?"

"Heavens no. I certainly wouldn't want to interfere with all these intricate plans you've been hatching. Will I see you before the ball?"

"I don't think it would be wise."

"Oops!" She snapped her fingers. "I forgot for a moment. Discretion is the name of the game."

His gaze narrowed on her face. "Why aren't you angry any longer?"

"Understanding banishes anger." A brilliant smile lit her face. "All you had to do was explain your position."

"And you'll be reasonable?"

"Very reasonable. What am I supposed to wear to this ball?"

"I've had a gown made for you."

Her eyes widened. "Then you must have been planning this for a long time."

"Since the time we took the *palacio*." He smiled faintly. "I would have brought you back here even if you hadn't been pregnant. Saint Pierre owes you a debt and we pay our debts. I hope you find the gown to your satisfaction."

She lifted a brow. "Will it fit?"

"It will fit. I gave the dressmaker the yellow robe you left behind. And if the gown needs to be let out, the seamstress here can do it." He paused. "You looked very beautiful in that robe."

"Señora Sardona's lovely hand-me-down. I liked it. I hope you got it back from the dressmaker."

He shook his head. "I didn't think you had any use for it."

"A woman can always use another robe." She smothered a yawn. "Can one of these stalwart guards at the door show me my quarters? Paco woke me up at three A.M. and I can't seem to get enough sleep these days."

"Yes." As she moved away from him, he took an impulsive step forward. "But I'll take you."

"Oh, no." She gazed up at him limpidly as she opened the door. "We wouldn't want to give the impression we're more than friends."

She sailed through the doorway and shut the door quietly behind her.

"You wanted to see me?" Paco asked as Lara opened the door of her suite at his knock.

She nodded, then stepped aside to let him in. "I have a few questions to ask."

Wariness flickered in Paco's expression. "I don't know if I can answer them."

"For Pete's sake, Paco, we've been through too much together for you to close up on me now. I need answers."

Paco didn't reply. His glance fell to the floor.

Lara drew a deep breath and then burst out, "Does he love me?"

"How should I know?"

Lara could see it was going to be like pulling teeth to get information from the man. "Has he ever talked about me?"

"No."

Disappointment surged through her. "Never?"

"Only to say you must be protected."

"Why did he send me away?"

Paco didn't answer.

"That day of the sniper attack he changed toward me in the blink of an eyelash. Dammit, he must have said something to you on the way back to the caverns."

"No." His gaze finally lifted to her face and he said reluctantly, "But he said something to Juan while he was bandaging his shoulder."

She held her breath.

"He said, 'The bullet went through my shoulder. An inch to the left and it would have blown Lara's brains out.' "

It was what she had suspected, what she had hoped for. Her breath escaped in a rush of air. "Thanks, Paco."

He shook his head. "I don't think it will do any good. He won't admit it, and he won't change his mind. He's seen too many friends and loved ones die over the years. He won't risk you." He gently touched her cheek with his forefinger. "I'm sorry, Lara."

"I'm not. I've got a weapon to fight with now. Before I had nothing. I didn't even know I had a battle to fight."

"Good luck." Paco turned to leave the suite. "I hope you win your battle."

"I don't see why I shouldn't." She grinned. "Haven't you heard? I'm a genuine, medal-sporting heroine, and a heroine always carries the day."

Nine

Dear heaven, she was nervous.

Lara smoothed the wide silk skirts of her ball gown and tried to breathe slowly and deeply. It was all very well to talk big and exude confidence before the fact, but now that the moment of truth had arrived, she could feel her confidence eroding. Standing in the hall waiting to go into the ballroom to accept that damn medal didn't make her any less upset.

"You look very beautiful," Paco said quietly in her ear. "The television cameramen will have a field day."

"It's the gown." The square-necked ball gown Ricardo's dressmaker had created for her was fashioned of a magnificent pink silk embroidered in a delicate floral design with glittering golden bugle beads. "I feel like Princess Di."

"Don't say that." Paco made a face. "You're a heroine of the Republic. We don't recognize royalty here on Saint Pierre."

"I'd rather not be recognized at all. Can't you go in and tell Ricardo I don't want the blasted medal?"

He shook his head. "You agreed to accept it. It will be over in just a few minutes. When your name is called, you and your escort cross the ballroom to the raised pedestal where Ricardo is standing and—"

"My escort? Those two men who got medals didn't have escorts."

"You're a woman."

"I think we need a feminist organization down here."

"Ricardo thought you might be nervous."

"Who, me?" She shivered. "I'm scared to death."

Paco smiled. "Then he was right."

"He has a tiresome habit of being right—well, sometimes. Are you going to escort me?"

"No, Ricardo has reserved that right for someone else. I have to meet a late arrival downstairs."

"If it's not going to be you, I'd rather go it alone."

Paco shook his head. "You'll feel quite comfortable with this escort." The door to the ballroom opened and he turned. "Here he is now."

Manuel stood in the doorway, dressed in a full dress army uniform, his black shoes shined to a high luster no brighter than his eyes. "You don't mind?" he asked Lara with quaint gravity. "It would be my very great honor to escort you."

Ricardo had done this. He had known how nervous Lara would feel and had sent the one person who would put her instantly at ease. She felt the tension leave her as she swept Manuel a curtsy and said gently as she took his arm, "And it would be my very great honor to accept your escort."

*   *   *

The medal was a green, white, and scarlet ribbon embellished with a golden sunburst medallion.

Ricardo slipped the ribbon over her head and then stepped back as the medallion nestled against the pink satin of her bodice. Flashbulbs went off somewhere in the background and she heard the click of camera shutters.

"The government of Saint Pierre gives thanks for your service, and honors your courage." Ricardo's tone was formal, stilted, and Lara did not receive the warm smile he had awarded the other two honorees.

She vaguely heard polite applause as she stepped off the raised pedestal and moved to the side to merge with the other guests at the ball. Ricardo immediately turned away and must have made some signal to indicate the awards ceremony was at an end, for the orchestra began to play again. "You did very well," Manuel said solemnly. "I was afraid you'd trip on the hem of your gown as we crossed the ballroom."

"I'm glad you didn't tell me before. I probably would have done just that." She heard a buzz of conversation from the elegantly dressed people surrounding her and received a few tentative smiles. She smiled automatically in return before she turned away. Now that the ceremony was over, she only wanted to escape. "Find me a way out of—"

"Quite a necklace. A little gaudy with that gown, but then you never did know how to coordinate an ensemble."

"Brett!" She whirled around to face her brother's teasing grin.

Paco stood behind Brett's wheelchair, a broad smile on his face. "Our late arrival. I told you I'd let him know you had a good reason for going to Saint Pierre."

Lara flew across the few yards separating her from Brett's wheelchair. "Are you okay? The trip wasn't too much for you?"

Brett grimaced. "The trip was fine. It was getting outfitted in these fancy duds that wore me out." He waved his hand at the tuxedo he wore. "I hope you appreciate the sacrifice I made just to see you get that fancy piece of jewelry."

"I appreciate it." Lara swallowed to ease the tightness in her throat. "They shouldn't have given it to me. You're the one who deserves it."

"I receive mine at the military ceremony next week. This is the glitz-and-glamour edition."

"Next week? You're not going back to Barbados?"

"I told you I was coming back to Saint Pierre. Paco found me a place in the hospital here. Afterward . . ." He shrugged. "Who knows?"

"There's always a place for you in Saint Pierre, Brett," Paco said. "As soon as we get you well, we'll find out where it is."

"Paco tells me you're leaving for the United States tomorrow." Brett smiled coaxingly at Lara. "I think it's very unkind of you to run away just when I've arrived here. Why don't you stick around and help ease your invalid brother in his hour of need?"

"I might do that." Lara lifted her gaze to meet Paco's over Brett's head. She smiled defiantly. "It would only be the sisterly thing to do; wouldn't it, Paco?"

"I understood it was most urgent you leave Saint Pierre at once," Paco said without expression.

"Did you?" Lara stepped behind Brett's wheelchair. "Run along, Paco. I know you have zillions of things to do. Manuel and I will just take Brett over to the buffet to sample those luscious-looking crab hors d'oeuvres."

"Lara." Paco's tone was warning

Lara ignored him as she and Manuel swept Brett across the floor to the buffet table across the ballroom.

She had forgotten about the two guards at the door of Ricardo's suite.

Dammit, why couldn't one of them have been Pedro, who had guarded Ricardo's quarters in the cavern? She could have used a break.

She stopped, tightened the belt of her yellow velvet robe, and marched regally down the hall toward them. *"Buenas tardes."*

They both nodded politely.

So far, so good. She smiled brightly as her hand went to the knob of the door.

Two rifles immediately formed a menacing cross in front of her face.

Wrong move. She smiled soothingly at them and knocked on the door instead of opening it. "Settle down. I'm not going to assassinate him. I just want—"

The door was flung open and Ricardo faced her. He had removed his uniform jacket and tie and wore only his white shirt, form-fitting uniform trousers, and shiny black boots. He stiffened. "What the hell are you doing here?"

"Trying to avoid being shot by these kind gentlemen." Lara gestured to the guards. "Maybe I should have worn my medal."

"It would have been a hell of a lot more discreet

than that robe," he said hoarsely as his gaze traveled over her. "You're ruining everything, dammit."

"Are you going to let me come in or are we going to argue in front of the—"

He grasped her arm and pulled her into the sitting room before she could finish the sentence. He slammed the door and whirled her around to face him. "I can't believe you did this. The *palacio* is still crawling with reporters. If anyone saw you, it could be in every tabloid in the world by morning."

"The guards saw me."

"I can take care of them. They won't speak or I'll—"

"Have their tongues cut out?" Lara clucked reprovingly. "I've heard power corrupts. You've just been inaugurated and already you're becoming as oppressive as the junta."

"My men are loyal to me. I wouldn't have to threaten them."

"But you probably would. You look very intimidating right now. I do believe you're letting emotion rule you." She grinned. "And, personally, I'm all for it." She took a step toward him and began to unbutton his white shirt. "I'm very tired of that formidable control of yours. It's getting in my way."

He looked down at her fingers undoing the buttons. "What are you doing?" he asked thickly.

"Isn't it obvious? I'm undressing you." She frowned. "And these little buttons are the devil. If you'd like to return the favor, I assure you that you won't have the same problem. I'm not wearing anything beneath the robe."

"I know." His gaze fastened on the clear delineation of her nipples pressing against the velvet and he unconsciously moistened his lower lip with his tongue. "What the hell are you trying to do to me?"

"Seduce you." She cast a glance at his lower body. "And, judging by appearances, I think I'm doing rather well." She parted the edges of his shirt, and her hands reached in to tangle with the hair on his chest. "Don't you?"

A shudder went through him.

She bent her head and her tongue licked delicately at the small hard nipple half covered by the dark springy thatch.

"Lord." The exclamation was a half-inaudible groan. He reached out and grasped her shoulders and began to draw her toward him. Then he stopped, his hands tightened painfully, and he pushed her away. "No."

"Yes." She swallowed. She had hoped it wouldn't be this difficult. She didn't know how to go about seducing a man. When they had come together before, it had always been a natural merging of passion, with both of them contributing equally to the fire. "You want it. I want it. Let it happen."

"I can't let it happen. I'm not an animal. I'm a thinking human being who is responsible for his actions." His hands closed into fists at his sides. "Why are you here?"

"Because I hate to lose."

"To stay here is the surest way to lose."

She would certainly lose if she stood and argued with him. It would be better to get him to physically commit before words got in the way. "I don't agree." She stepped closer to him and rubbed against him, letting him feel the sensuous flow of velvet and warm flesh.

He gasped and shuddered again.

She didn't know how long she could go on. She

was beginning to tremble herself. He was too close. It had been too long. She could feel a hot tingling between her thighs. "I've thought about it and decided I want to be *el presidente's* mistress and have his covey of children after all." She rubbed her cheek back and forth on his chest. "Will you give me another medal if I have twins? They run in the family, you know."

"Stop joking. I can't do—" He broke off as her hand slid slowly beneath his waistband and down his muscular belly. "Lara, be sensible."

"I can't be sensible." Her voice was muffled against his chest. "I love you."

He went still.

"You never let me say it, but I think you knew that day at the lake."

He drew a deep, harsh breath. "And what am I supposed to do about it?"

"You're supposed to make love to me so I won't feel like such a klutz standing here making the most important confession of my life."

"I can't tell you I love—"

"I said *make* love," she said fiercely as she looked up at him with tear-bright eyes. "I don't want words. All I want is tonight. One night, dammit. Is that too much to ask?"

He hesitated before a brilliant smile lit his dark face with tender radiance. "Then I'll give you what you want." He lifted her up and carried her into the bedroom. "You won't lose tonight, *querida*." He laid her gently on the enormous bed, shrugged out of his shirt, and lay down beside her. "And neither will I."

* * *

"Where did you get the robe?" Ricardo asked idly as he brushed a kiss on her cheek. "I gave it to the dressmaker for sizing."

"I went into town after it." She lifted herself on her elbow and looked down at him. "I thought I'd need every bit of seductive power I could muster to get the great liberator to take me to bed." She grinned. "You were easier than I thought you'd be."

He stiffened. "Not so easy. I only promised you one night."

"I lied. I want the whole ball game."

"We can't have it."

"Sure we can. You just have to give us a chance."

"We've had our chance. In the morning you leave with Paco for the United States."

"The devil I do."

He gazed up at her. "Tonight meant nothing of importance. I don't want you as my mistress and I don't love you, Lara."

His expression was sincere, his words ringing with truth, and for an instant Lara believed him. Then she remembered his voice echoing over and over behind her as Jurado's whip had lashed her.

She means nothing to me.

He had lied to Jurado; now he was lying to her and for the same reason. He had become a master at hiding his emotions over the years and he had almost deceived her, as he had that day of the sniper attack. She would not let him bluff her into giving up so easily this time.

She had still not won the battle.

But she had won enough for now. She leaned forward and gently kissed his lips. "It's all right," she whispered. "Don't worry about it. I'm not going to push you into saying you care about me." She lifted his hand to her lips and kissed the palm lingeringly. "But can't you at least tell me you like making love to me?" She put his hand on her breast. "Just to give a woman a little encouragement?"

He stared at her, a multitude of emotions conflicting on his face. His hand reached up to cup her cheek with a touch so gentle, it was a tender blessing. "Oh, yes." He suddenly jerked her down, flipped her over, and plunged deep within her. An expression of almost painful pleasure appeared on his face. "There's no question. I definitely love this."

"Lara."

Lara opened her eyes to see Paco's face above her. This was getting to be a habit, she thought drowsily. But it wasn't dark, as it had been in her bedroom in Barbados. The strong morning sunlight poured through the French window across the room. Ricardo's room. Paco shouldn't be in Ricardo's bedroom, she realized vaguely.

"Lara, wake up."

Lara glanced at the pillow next to her own. Empty. The pillow showed the indentation of Ricardo's head, but Ricardo was gone. The knowledge shocked her awake and she sat upright in bed. "Where is he?"

"Gone." Paco reached down and quickly pulled up the silken coverlet to cover her bare breasts. She absently grasped it, her gaze searching Paco's expression as he continued, "He came to my quarters at dawn and left the *palacio* shortly afterward."

"Left for where?"

"I've had your bags packed. Ricardo wants you off Saint Pierre by the time he returns."

The battle had resumed with a vengeance.

"Then he'd better be prepared to be gone for a hell of a long time because he's going to have to run the blasted country from exile. I'm not leaving." She ran her fingers through her hair, struggling against tears. "I should have talked sense into him when I had him, dammit. How was I supposed to know he'd run out on me when—" She swung her feet to the floor, winding the spread around her like an Indian blanket. "Where's my robe? I've got to get out of here." She saw the robe on the floor, snatched it up, and headed for the bathroom. "Send to my room for my clothes will you, Paco?"

"Ricardo doesn't want anyone to know you're here in his suite."

"Then please get them yourself, while I shower. I have to go after him."

Paco shook his head. "He's my commander in chief and the president of my country. I'm under orders to escort you to the United States."

"He's also your friend, dammit." Lara glanced over her shoulder. "I can't let him go now. You know how strong he is. I can't give him the chance to rebuild the barriers I tore down last night." She whispered, "Please don't make me go, Paco."

He hesitated and then sighed resignedly. "He'll probably court-martial me for disobeying orders."

"No, he won't. The grounds for prosecution would bring me into the public eye and that's what he's trying to avoid."

He smiled faintly. "True."

She turned at the door of the bathroom. "Where is he?"

"He went home."

"Home? I thought the *palacio* was home now."

Paco shook his head. "Home has always been the rancho to Ricardo. The government officially returned the property to him after the junta was defeated."

"Where is it?"

"About seventy-five miles south of the city."

"Will you take me there?"

"Why not? I can't get into any more trouble than I'm in already."

"Thanks, Paco."

"De nada." Paco paused. "It's your last chance, Lara. I can't disobey Ricardo again. Are you sure you want to try this? I've never seen him more determined."

"He's crumbling." She worriedly bit her lower lip. "Lord, I hope he's crumbling. That damn control . . . Why does he have to be so strong?"

"That strength is the only quality that kept him alive for the last ten years."

"I know. I know. I know it all." She turned and flung open the door of the bathroom. "The Pied Piper, *El Grande Libertador*, the legend."

Ten

Bright-red tiles roofed the large white stucco casa and wrought iron ornamental bars protected the windows on the upper level.

"Don't you recognize the ornamental bars your father placed on the windows to keep out suitors?"

Ricardo had given her his own home, drawn from his memories, to comfort her that night in the cell.

"It's exactly the same," she whispered.

"What?" Paco bypassed the *casa* and stables and parked the jeep outside the white stucco walls beside a Mercedes flying the national flag of Saint Pierre.

"Never mind."

Paco glanced at the shuttered *casa.* "The house looks as if it's deserted."

"I don't think he'll be in the house." She jumped out of the jeep. "Where's the lake?"

"About a quarter of a mile over that hill." He gestured to a rise to the south. "Do you want me to drive you?"

She shook her head. "I need time to think."

He got out of the car and leaned on the front bumper. "Then I'll wait here for you."

He didn't think she would be able to persuade Ricardo and was prepared to wait to pick up the pieces. Dear heaven, she hoped he was wrong.

She nodded in acknowledgment and set off quickly up the hill. She was shaking, she realized without surprise. She felt more nervous now than that first day Jurado had dragged her across the courtyard of the Abbey to the cell block where Ricardo Lázaro had been imprisoned.

Ricardo's rancho was as beautiful as the word picture he had drawn for her in the cell. Her gaze wandered over lush green foliage, wide pampalike pastures, rolling hills, and bright-petaled wildflowers. Peace.

She crested the hill, and the small lake lay in the valley before her—a small gem of a lake surrounded by tall grass and cypress trees.

Ricardo stood on the bank, gazing unseeingly down at the white water lilies floating on the water.

"There are water lilies floating on the lake and my Labrador is racing along the bank chasing a squirrel."

Ricardo wore dark trousers and a white linen shirt, and Lara felt a curious sense of shock as she looked at him. It was the first time she had seen him in anything but a military uniform. He somehow appeared less stern, more vulnerable in the civilian apparel. Vulnerable . . . and lonely.

She started down the hill.

He must have sensed her presence, for his head swiftly lifted and he glanced over his shoulder. She saw him stiffen as he saw her approaching only a few hundred yards away. She murmured a prayer under her breath.

"It's just the same," she called. "Just the way I pictured it. The *casa*, the ornamental bars, the lake. Only your big Labrador is missing."

"Jaime is dead. They're all dead."

Lord, she had blundered already. The last thing she had wanted was to remind him of all he had lost.

"How did you get here?" he asked.

"Paco brought me. He thinks you're going to murder him." She stopped before him. "I told him I'd protect him from you."

Every muscle in his body looked as rigid as if it had turned to stone; his face was expressionless. "And who's going to protect you from me? I would have thought you'd be able to take a hint. It's over, Lara."

"You know me. I'm as stubborn as they come. I don't take hints."

"How can I make it any plainer? I don't want you; I don't want your child; I don't want—"

"Oh, shut up." Her hands closed into fists at her sides as the tears rose helplessly to her eyes. "I'm tired of hearing you give me that bull. You love me. I know it, dammit." Oh, Lord, she hoped she was right. "You love me and you want me."

He was silent—as strong and guarded as an impregnable fortress.

Crumble. Please crumble.

Lara took a step closer "You're so damn stupid. Don't you know what we could have together? We love each other and we're going to have a child. You wanted to have someone to belong to you and now you have the whole shooting match." She closed her eyes. "Wrong phrase. Oh, dear, I can't say anything right. I wasn't going to remind you of guns and shooting. I know that's what set you off the day the sniper shot you."

"He almost killed you," Ricardo said hoarsely.

Her eyes flicked open as hope stirred. Ricardo's face was still expressionless, but there had been a note of raw pain in his voice.

"He was aiming at you. You're the one who got the bullet through the shoulder. Have you noticed me shoving you away because that might happen again? I'm more selfish than that. I'm going to grab whatever happiness I can and stick close to you and make sure I keep anything away that can hurt you or—"

"Sometimes you can't keep harm away. Sometimes, no matter how many precautions you take, it happens anyway."

"Then we'll have to face it."

He shook his head.

She felt a wild burst of panic, and the tears that had been brimming overflowed and ran down her cheeks. "Don't shake your head at me. You *love* me. Say it." She took a step forward and grabbed his shoulders and shook him. "I'm hurting, dammit. Tell me."

His fingers reached out to touch the dampness of her cheeks. "Oh, Lord," he said hoarsely. "Don't you see? I can't say it. I can't let anything happen to you."

"I don't see anything. I'm not your mother or your father; I'm not all the friends you've lost over the years; I'm not your dog, Jaime. I'm me! This is my choice." She shook him again. "You say everyone has the right to choose, but you're taking away the most important choice in my life. I won't let you do that."

"Please stop crying. It . . . hurts me."

"Do you think I'm not hurting? I'm bleeding inside." She looked up at him. "I've tried persistence, seduction, and reason, and none of it is getting through to you. And I know I shouldn't be getting this upset right now. Our baby will probably be born with a hideously bad temper and be—"

"As stubborn as his mother," Ricardo said huskily.

"I have to be stubborn. You won't listen to me. Well, I'm not going away. Do you hear me? You'll have to put me in the Abbey again to keep me away from you."

"I burned the Abbey to the ground."

"I forgot. Well, I'll follow you around barefoot and pregnant and ruin your image."

"I don't give a damn about my image."

"You care about Saint Pierre. That's all you do care about." She shook him again. "No, you care about me too. I know you do. Crumble, dammit."

"Crumble?"

"Like the walls of Jericho. Be strong with someone else. Fight with someone else. I'm on your side."

"If you'd stop shaking me and let me say something, you'd see that I've already crumbled."

She froze. "You have?" Her gaze searched his face. He was smiling, his face illuminated with the tenderness she knew so well. "You have!"

He took her in his arms and held her with exquisite gentleness. "How can I help it? I can't have you running around the streets barefoot and pregnant. It would offend both Manuel and Paco's sense of proper behavior worthy of a first lady."

"Don't joke." She wound her arms around him, and her words were muffled by his shirt. "I'm feeling very insecure. I need cosseting and reassurance."

"I love you, Lara." His voice broke on her name and his arms tightened about her. "Too much."

"There's no such thing as too much."

"I should let you go."

"Let? I thought I'd made it clear you'd have to hog-tie me, take away my passport, and close the borders to make me go." Happiness ran through her in an exultant stream. She felt drunk with relief and joy. "I'm here for the long haul."

"Lord, you're stubborn."

"I hate to lose. I would have been lost myself if I'd let you win this one."

"I'm not so sure. You won't be able to have what you want out of life." He pushed her away from him. "No small town, no lake, no—"

"I can have a dog," she said lightly. "I'll get myself a mutt as big as an Irish wolf hound, buy him a jeweled collar, and flaunt him among the rich and famous."

"I'm serious. I can't even give you this right now." He gestured to the lake. "My place is at the *palacio* and you'd have to live there too. If we lived apart, I couldn't provide you and the child with the security measures I'd feel comfortable with."

She made a face. "Why do I feel we're going to be tripping over bodyguards even in the bedroom?"

He suddenly smiled. "Perhaps not in the bedroom but everywhere else." His smile faded. "I'm terrified of you dying. I *won't* lose you."

"No, you won't lose me and I damn well won't lose you. And, as for the cottage . . ." She shrugged. "It can wait."

He kissed her. "Yes, it can wait."

"And when I feel I need to get away from the *palacio*, I can come to you as I did in the cell and you can tell me about the rancho and we can pretend. . . . Maybe imagination is better than reality anyway."

"Not for us." Ricardo said. "Not from now on." His index finger gently touched one tear-wet lash. " 'Bramble dew.' "

"That poem you quoted me," she identified. "My eyes are swollen and I'm sniffing like a baby. I can't imagine anyone comparing me to the heroine in a poem at the moment."

He nodded. "There's one more verse to it, you know."

She tilted her head and gazed at him curiously. "Why didn't you recite it before?"

"You wouldn't even say you loved me at the time and I was afraid I'd scare you away."

She chuckled as she remembered her impassioned pursuit of Ricardo for the past two days. "That seems like a very long time ago. Everything has turned around. My, how the mighty have fallen."

"Crumbled," Ricardo corrected, his dark eyes twinkling.

She nodded. "Crumbled. What's the last verse?"

He smiled, his expression loving as he quoted softly,

"Teacher, tender comrade, wife,
A fellow-farer true through life,
Heart-whole and soul-free,
The August Father gave to me."

THE EDITOR'S CORNER

In publishing a series such as LOVESWEPT we couldn't function without timetables, schedules, deadlines. It seems we're always working toward one, only to reach it then strive for another. I mention the topic because many of you write and ask us questions about the way we work and about how and when certain books are published. Just consider this Editor's Corner as an example. I'm writing this in early April, previewing our October books, which will run in our September books, which will be on sale in August. The books you're reading about were scheduled for publication at least nine months earlier and were probably written more than a year before they reach your hands! Six books a month means seventy-two a year, and we're into our seventh year of publication. That's a lot of books and a lot of information to try to keep up with. Amazingly, we do keep up—and so do our authors. We enjoy providing you with the answer to a question about a particular book or author or character. Your letters mean a lot to us.

In our ongoing effort to extend the person-to-person philosophy of LOVESWEPT, we are setting up a 900 number through which you can learn what's new—and what's old—with your favorite authors! Next month's Editor's Corner will have the full details for you.

Kay Hooper's most successful series for us to date has been her *Once Upon a Time . . .* novels. These modern-day fairy tales have struck a chord with you, the readers, and your enjoyment of the books has delighted and inspired Kay. Her next in this series is LOVESWEPT #426, **THE LADY AND THE LION,** and it's one of Kay's sizzlers. Keith Donovan and Erin Prentice first speak to each other from their adjacent hotel balconies, sharing secrets and desperate murmurings in the dark. Kay creates a moody, evocative, emotionally charged atmosphere in which these two kindred spirits fall in love before they ever meet. But when they finally do set eyes on each other, they know without having to speak that they've found their destinies. This wonderful story will bring out the true romantic in all of you!

We take you from fairy tales to fairyland this month! Our next LOVESWEPT, #427, **SATIN SHEETS AND STRAWBERRIES** by Marcia Evanick, features a golden-haired nymph of a heroine named Kelli SantaFe. Hero Logan Sinclair does a double take when he arrives at what looks like Snow White's cottage in search of his aunt and uncle—and finds a bewitching woman dressed as a fairy. Kelli runs her business from her home and at first resents Logan's interference and the tug-of-war he wages for his relatives, whom she'd taken in and treated like the family

(continued)

she'd always wanted. Logan is infuriated by her stubbornness, yet intrigued by the woman who makes him feel as though his feet barely touch the ground. Kelli falls hard for Logan, who can laugh at himself and rescue damsels in distress, but who has the power to shatter her happiness. You'll find yourself be enchanted by the time Kelli and Logan discover how to weave their dreams together!

All of us feel proud and excited whenever we publish a new author in the line. The lady whose work we're introducing you to next month is a talented, hardworking mother of five who strongly believes in the importance of sprinkling each day with a little romance. We think Olivia Rupprecht does just that with **BAD BOY OF NEW ORLEANS**, LOVESWEPT #428. I don't know about you, but some of my all-time favorite romances involve characters who reunite after years apart. I find these stories often epitomize the meaning of true love. Well, in **BAD BOY OF NEW ORLEANS** Olivia reunites two people whose maddening hunger for each other has only deepened with time. Hero Chance Renault can still make Micah Sinclair tremble, can still make her burn for his touch and cry out for the man who had loved her first. But over time they've both changed, and a lot stands between them. Micah feels she must prove she can survive on her own, while Chance insists she belongs to him body and soul. Their journey toward happiness together is one you won't want to miss!

Joan Elliott Pickart never ceases to amaze me with the way she is able to provide us with winning romance after winning romance. She's truly a phenomenon, and we're pleased and honored to bring you her next LOVESWEPT, #429, **STORMING THE CASTLE**. While reunited lovers have their own sets of problems to overcome, when two very different people find themselves falling in love, their long-held beliefs, values, and lifestyles become an issue. In **STORMING THE CASTLE**, Dr. Maggie O'Leary finds her new hunk of a neighbor, James-Steven Payton, to be a free spirit, elusive as the wind and just as irresistible. Leave it to him to choose the unconventional over the customary way of doing things. But Maggie grew up with a father who was much the same, whose devil-may-care ways often brought heartache. James-Steven longs to see the carefree side of Maggie, and he sets out to get her to smell the flowers and to build sand castles without worrying that the tide will wash them away. Though Maggie longs to join her heart to his, she knows they must first find a common ground. Joan handles this tender story beautifully. It's a real heart-warmer!

One author who always delivers a fresh, innovative story is Mary Kay McComas. Each of her LOVESWEPTs is unique and imaginative—never the same old thing! In **FAVORS**, LOVESWEPT #430, Mary Kay has once again let her creative juices flow, and

(continued)

the result is a story unlike any other. Drawing on her strength in developing characters you come to know intimately and completely, Mary Kay serves up a romance filled with emotion and chock full of fun. Her tongue-in-cheek portrayal of several secondary characters will have you giggling, and her surprise ending will add the finishing touch to your enjoyment of the story. When agent Ian Walker is asked to protect a witness as a favor to his boss, he considers the job no more appealing than baby-sitting—until he meets Trudy Babbitt, alias Pollyanna. The woman infuriates him by refusing to believe she's in danger—and ignites feelings in him he'd thought were long dead. Trudy sees beneath Ian's crusty exterior and knows she can transform him with her love. But first they have to deal with the reality of their situation. I don't want to give away too much, so I'll just suggest you keep in mind while reading **FAVORS** that nothing is exactly as it seems. Crafty Mary Kay pulls a few aces from her sleeve!

One of your favorite authors—and ours—Billie Green returns to our lineup next month with **SWEET AND WILDE**, #431. Billie has always been able to capture that indefinable quality that makes a LOVESWEPT romance special. In her latest for us, she throws together an unlikely pair of lovers, privileged Alyson Wilde and streetwise Sid Sweet and sends them on an incredible adventure. You might wonder what a blue-blooded lady could have in common with a bail bondsman and pawnshop owner, but Billie manages to keep her characters more than a little bit interested in each other. When thirteen-year-old Lenny, who is Alyson's ward, insists that his friend Sid Sweet is a great guy and role model, Alyson decides she has to meet the tough-talking man for herself. And cynical Sid worries that Good Samaritan Alyson has taken Lenny on only as her latest "project." With Lenny's best interests at heart, they go with him in search of his past and end up discovering their own remarkable future—one filled with a real love that is better than any of their fantasies.

Be sure to pick up all six books next month. They're all keepers!

Sincerely,

Susann Brailey

Susann Brailey
Editor
LOVESWEPT
Bantam Books
666 Fifth Avenue
New York, NY 10103

FAN OF THE MONTH

Sandra Beattie

How did I come to be such a fan of LOVESWEPT romances? It was by accident, really. My husband was in the Australian Navy and we were moving once again to another state. I wanted some books to read while we stayed in the motel, so I went to a second-hand bookstore in search of some Silhouette romances. I spotted some books I hadn't seen before, and after reading the back covers I decided to buy two. I asked the saleslady to set the rest aside in case I wanted them later. I read both books that night and was hooked. I raced back to the store the next day and bought the rest. I've been a fan of LOVESWEPT ever since.

My favorite authors are Sandra Brown, Kay Hooper, Iris Johansen, Fayrene Preston, Joan Elliott Pickart, and Mary Kay McComas. The thing I like about LOVESWEPT heroes is that they are not always rich and handsome men, but some are struggling like us. I cry and laugh with the people in the books. Sometimes I become them and feel everything that they feel. The love scenes are just so romantic that they take my breath away. But then some of them are funny as well.

I'm thirty-four years old, the mother of three children. I love rock and roll, watching old movies, and snuggling up to my husband on cold, rainy nights. If there is one thing I can pass on to other readers, it is that you can't let everything get you down. When I feel depressed, I pick up a LOVESWEPT and curl up in a chair for a while and just forget about everything. Then when I get up again, the world doesn't look so bad anymore. Try it, it really works!

60 Minutes to a Better, More Beautiful You!

Now it's easier than ever to awaken your sensuality, stay slim forever—even make yourself irresistible. With Bantam's bestselling subliminal audio tapes, you're only 60 minutes away from a better, more beautiful you!

__	45004-2	**Slim Forever**	$8.95
__	45112-X	**Awaken Your Sensuality**	$7.95
__	45035-2	**Stop Smoking Forever**	$8.95
__	45130-8	**Develop Your Intuition**	$7.95
__	45022-0	**Positively Change Your Life**	$8.95
__	45154-5	**Get What You Want**	$7.95
__	45041-7	**Stress Free Forever**	$8.95
__	45106-5	**Get a Good Night's Sleep**	$7.95
__	45094-8	**Improve Your Concentration**	$7.95
__	45172-3	**Develop A Perfect Memory**	$8.95

Bantam Books, Dept. LT, 414 East Golf Road, Des Plaines, IL 60016

Please send me the items I have checked above. I am enclosing $_____
(please add $2.00 to cover postage and handling). Send check or money order, no cash or C.O.D.s please. (Tape offer good in USA only.)

Mr/Ms _____

Address _____

City/State_____ Zip_____

LT-5/90

Please allow four to six weeks for delivery.
Prices and availability subject to change without notice.

THE SHAMROCK TRINITY

☐ **21975 RAFE, THE MAVERICK**
  by Kay Hooper $2.95

☐ **21976 YORK, THE RENEGADE**
  by Iris Johansen $2.95

☐ **21977 BURKE, THE KINGPIN**
  by Fayrene Preston $2.95